"Don't look at me lik

She raised her gaze to his.

His fingers tightened in her hair and her mouth ran dry. She swallowed. Moistened her lips.

She wasn't sure if she moved first. Or if it was him.

But then his mouth was on hers and she felt engulfed by his heat. Or maybe the burning was coming from inside her.

There was no way to know.

No reason to care.

Her hands slid up the granite chest, behind his neck, where his skin felt even hotter beneath her fingertips, and slipped through his thick hair, which was not hot, but instead felt cool and unexpectedly silky.

His arm around her tightened, his hand pressing her closer while his kiss deepened. Consuming. Exhilarating. Her head whirled with roaring sounds.

It was only a kiss.

But she was melting.

She was flying.

And then she realized the sounds weren't just inside her head.

Someone was laying on a horn.

RETURN TO THE DOUBLE C:
Under the big blue Wyoming sky,
this family discovers true love!

Dear Reader,

I always love going back to Weaver, where everything started for the Clay family. But I've returned so often that sometimes I wonder what else can possibly happen there.

Well, it turns out that a lot *is* happening!

April Reed wasn't strictly a child of the Double C, but she's family nevertheless. Now she's back on behalf of her developer boss to wrangle a deal over the mountain that overlooks the town. It's not as simple as it could be. Nothing at all about her visit to Weaver turns out to be. Particularly when she meets a loner named Jed Dalloway, who is keeping watch over a small ranch on the mountain.

Family troubles. Overcoming pasts. Discovering hope. Most of all, finding love when you least expect it.

All that and more is Weaver. It's what I love about the place and I hope you'll love it, too.

Allison

A Promise to Keep

Allison Leigh

HARLEQUIN
SPECIAL
EDITION

ISBN-13: 978-1-335-89440-3

A Promise to Keep

Copyright © 2020 by Allison Lee Johnson

Recycling programs
for this product may
not exist in your area.

This is a work of fiction. Names, characters, places and incidents
are either the product of the author's imagination or are used fictitiously.
Any resemblance to actual persons, living or dead, businesses,
companies, events or locales is entirely coincidental.

This edition published by arrangement with Harlequin Books S.A.

For questions and comments about the quality of this book,
please contact us at CustomerService@Harlequin.com.

Harlequin Enterprises ULC
22 Adelaide St. West, 40th Floor
Toronto, Ontario M5H 4E3, Canada
www.Harlequin.com

Printed in U.S.A.

Though her name is frequently on bestseller lists, **Allison Leigh**'s high point as a writer is hearing from readers that they laughed, cried or lost sleep while reading her books. She credits her family with great patience for the time she's parked at her computer, and for blessing her with the kind of love she wants her readers to share with the characters living in the pages of her books. Contact her at allisonleigh.com.

Books by Allison Leigh

Harlequin Special Edition

Return to the Double C

A Weaver Christmas Gift
One Night in Weaver...
The BFF Bride
A Child Under His Tree
Yuletide Baby Bargain
Show Me a Hero
The Rancher's Christmas Promise
A Promise to Keep

Montana Mavericks: 20 Years in the Saddle!

Destined for the Maverick

The Fortunes of Texas: The Rulebreakers

Fortune's Homecoming

The Fortunes of Texas: The Secret Fortunes

Wild West Fortune

The Fortunes of Texas: All Fortune's Children

Fortune's Secret Heir

Visit the Author Profile page
at Harlequin.com for more titles.

For my family.

Chapter One

The house—a generous term if there ever was one—sat on the side of the mountain. The wood had gone gray with weathering and the windows were miserly in number as well as size—probably to keep out the cold. Even on the warmest of summer days, there would be the wind that never, ever seemed to let up.

Summer hadn't hit this part of Wyoming yet. During this time of year—well, March to May, pretty much—it could be warm one day and a blizzard the next. Squarely in the middle of April—the month after which she was named—it was colder than a witch's tongue and a foot of snow still clung in the shadows.

Which meant the wind was sharper and more stinging than ever, and from the moment April Reed left the warmth of her car's heated interior, it furiously whipped her hair straight into her eyes as she squinted up at the mountain.

Up at the odd-angled, wood-sided house.

It had to be constructed of sterner stuff than it appeared, or it would have blown off Rambling Mountain long, long ago. Either that or it was a testament to the sheer stubbornness of the house's occupant.

Her grandfather, Squire Clay, had always said that nobody was more stubborn than Otis Lambert. Not even Squire, himself.

Which was saying something.

She pulled the collar of her leather coat against her throat and reached inside the car for her briefcase. When she straightened, the wind slammed the car door shut for her. She yanked the edge of her jacket free where it had caught and squinted into the wind as she moved past a dusty blue pickup and stepped around the wooden barricade blocking the road leading up to the weather-beaten house. Even without the barricade, she wouldn't have been able to drive the last half mile up to the house. Not with the rockslide. The boulders weren't enough to block passage entirely, but they were definitely enough to block a vehicle.

She chewed the inside of her cheek as she weaved

her way around a four-wheeler parked on the other side of the blockage and glanced back down the road. Developing the road would be costly. When she was finished meeting with Lambert, she'd take some photos of the damage and email them to her boss. Gage Stanton wasn't likely to let a few boulders stand in his way, but he'd still want a general sense of what they'd be facing. Ultimately, her boss had in mind a sumptuous resort catering to outdoor enthusiasts, because Rambling Mountain could offer it all. Rock climbing. Hunting. Fishing. Whatever. The only road on the mountain was this one. It would need to be passable even if Gage chose another location on the mountain for the resort.

The wind whistled and she pulled her collar close again, turning to head up the road. It was steep. Treacherously narrow. She instinctively moved away from the side that overlooked the sheer drop-off. Hundreds of feet below glistened a pristine lake fed by natural underground springs. A lake that would provide endless recreational opportunities. If a person could reach it.

It might seem strange for one person to own an entire mountain, but one did.

Otis Lambert.

Technically, water was the property of the state, but Lambert and his ancestors had always exercised their water rights when it came to the lake. It wasn't that they'd unreasonably withheld the natural stream water that flowed from it. Down the mountain, that water helped irrigate the region, including the town of Weaver and a whole lot of ranch land. But the only accessible point to the lake from a recreational standpoint lay entirely within Otis Lambert's property. Thousands and thousands of acres of it.

And one week ago, Otis had contacted her boss, Gage Stanton. Founder of Stanton Development. A Colorado-based company known for everything from award-winning, master-planned communities to hospitals to amusement parks.

The very fact that Otis had requested a meeting with a developer would seem to imply that he was softening when it came to sharing his mountain.

"Won't happen, girl."

Her grandfather's words from just that morning swam in her mind. They'd been sitting at the round oak table in the middle of the kitchen at the big house. The stack of golden waffles that her grandmother, Gloria, had set on the table had been quickly decimated by Squire and her uncle Matthew. He was Squire's son and had run the Double-C for as long as April could remember.

And all four of them—Squire and Gloria, Matthew and his wife, Jaimie—lived together in the sprawling old house everyone referred to as the "big house." As one of the largest cattle operations in the state of Wyoming as well as several states beyond, the Double-C commanded considerable influence and wealth. Considering that, the big house was actually somewhat modest in size. And even though Squire was supposedly retired as the head of the ranch, he could still ride and rope as well as any one of his progeny and he'd never stopped looking for an opportunity to add to their holdings.

"Won't happen, girl," he'd said, his icy blue eyes squinting at her as he sipped his steaming coffee from a china cup. "I've spent more 'n half my life trying to negotiate a deal with Lambert to connect those two sections o' land we own down on the southwest corner. Old hermit isn't even willin' to discuss leasing a couple hunnert acres that he'd never miss. The man's sitting on millions but he lives like a pauper 'cause that's the way he likes it. Waste of time goin' up the mountain to see him. Be better off tryin' to sell ice to a glacier."

"Stop trying to discourage her," Gloria had chided as she gave April a quick wink. "Not everyone is as stubborn as you. Maybe Otis'll have a soft spot for a red-haired girl."

Squire had grunted at that, a faint smile on his lips. "Well, I guess that worked for me back when you were a nurse poking me with needles 'n naggin' me about drinking my coffee."

"Keeping you alive," Matthew had reminded his father as he pushed away from the table and dropped a kiss on Jaimie's head. "Everyone's heard

*that Lambert's sick. Really sick. You're just aggra-
vated that your granddaughter's beating you to the
punch getting a meeting with him."*

*Squire had made a face, but his eyes, which
could look cold as winter, had been warm and kind
as he'd eyed her. "Do your best, girl. But be prepared for disappointment. Lambert's never shared
an inch of land. Sick or not, can't see him changing now."*

Loose gravel slid under April's boot and she
barely caught herself from landing on her knee.
Cussing under her breath, she stopped still and
hauled in a deep breath. If she'd known she'd be
having this hike ahead of her, she would have worn
more suitable boots.

She looked back down again toward her red car,
then up toward the house. She'd only gone halfway.
Even though she was accustomed to living with
elevation—Denver wasn't called the Mile High City
for nothing—the air was even thinner up here and
the ramshackle house wasn't situated anywhere near
the summit.

She knew why Gage had sent her to take the appointment with Lambert. She may have grown up
mostly in Arizona, but she'd still spent plenty of
time in Wyoming. Visiting her grandparents for
holidays, spending summers there. Her boss had
sent her, ostensibly, because she had an edge, being
"sort of" a local girl.

She knew it was more than that, though. If Lambert's health were really as bad as it was rumored, there'd be a lot of interested parties where his land was concerned. And first in line would be her grandfather, Squire Clay. The only thing more important than that land was his family. If April could successfully negotiate a deal with Lambert now, it was guaranteed that Squire wouldn't try to get in the way.

There was good reason Gage was so successful.

She swiped her hair away again, took another deep breath and set off once more.

She hadn't gone twenty yards before a figure appeared from behind the house. He was too far away to make out his features, but his stride wasn't slowed at all as he kicked through a mound of snow, aiming her way.

It wasn't the sight of the man that was alarming, particularly. She'd never met Otis Lambert. Never seen him before, even. But this man's head was bare and she doubted Otis—who, like Squire, was somewhere in his nineties—had a full head of dark hair.

Which meant he was the ranch hand. Jed Dalloway.

Otis had taken him on several years back, according to Squire. And he was almost as reclusive as Otis.

No, the man didn't alarm her. But the fierce dog at the man's side, curling back its lips to expose wickedly sharp teeth, was another matter.

She was used to dogs. Liked them. The only reason she didn't have one herself was that she lived in a loft apartment in downtown Denver and spent more hours at the office than she did at home. She couldn't give a dog the attention it deserved.

But this shaggy gray growling beast looked more wolf than dog.

A wolf had once come down from the mountains at the Double-C, picking off cattle along the way until Matthew and his brothers had gone out with a rifle to take care of it. She'd been sixteen at the time and full of outrage toward them.

Now she felt more like the poor cow must have felt, finding itself in a wolf's stare.

She lifted her chin, swiping the hair away from her eyes yet again. "Does he bite?" She'd raised her voice, but the wind nearly tore it away.

The man was coming toward her, the dog keeping pace. "What'd you say?"

The closer man and dog drew, the faster her heart beat. He was a good thirty feet away when he stopped. The denim shirt he wore open over a white T-shirt strained at his wide shoulders and yanked in the wind. The dog leaned against the side of his muddy jeans, teeth still bared. The growl was no longer imagined, but perfectly, nerve-rackingly audible.

It took every speck of willpower she had not to take a step back. "I asked if he bites."

"When he needs to."

She swiped at her hair again. Dragged her focus from the fearsome canine to the man. His eyes were narrowed. Unwelcoming.

But she had a reason to be there and wasn't going to be cowed just because a man gave her a narrow-eyed look. "That's not exactly a comforting answer."

"Wasn't intending it to be." But he lowered a raw-knuckled hand and touched the dog's head. The animal promptly sank down on its haunches. The growl ceased, though the teeth remained visible. "You're trespassing. Signs are posted on the road. The *private* road. You ignored them."

She tightened her grip on the leather strap of her briefcase. She'd never been a ninny and she wasn't starting now. She stepped toward him. "I'm not trespassing. I was invited. I'm April Reed with Stanton Development. I have an appointment with Mr. Lambert."

His eyes narrowed even more. If it weren't for the frown lines creasing his forehead and drawing down his lips, he might have been a nice-looking man in a rustic sort of way. "Otis isn't available."

She stopped. "Are you *his* guard dog like this one—" she waved her fingers toward the dog "—seems to be yours?"

His frown seemed to lighten a little, which didn't explain why her heart pounded even more nervously.

Nevertheless, he stayed hostile. "You've wasted a trip." He turned on his heel and the dog followed suit.

She gaped as he started walking back toward the house. She set off after him. "Wait! Hold on!"

She read impatience in the way his wide shoulders moved. The way he stopped, yet took a moment before turning toward her. When he did, his frown was firmly in place. She was close enough now to see his eyes were dark, though she couldn't tell what color of dark.

"You're Jed, right? Jed Dalloway?"

He didn't answer. Just kept looking at her with those dark, soulless eyes as she continued walking toward him, finally drawing even with him. With the chunky high heels of her leather boots, she stood close to six feet tall. He was still taller.

"I assure you, Mr. Dalloway, that your boss *is* expecting me." Projecting assurance had never felt quite as challenging as it did just then. She forced a small smile as she stepped past him, angling toward the weathered deck lining the front side of the house, as yet still several hundred feet away.

The deck was cantilevered over the cliff side. And looked to her pretty much like a death trap.

"Guess you're the reason he left, then."

She looked back at him. "He's not here?"

Jed gave a brief shrug.

She eyed him suspiciously. Tried to ferret some

hint of anything from his expression. "I understood that Mr. Lambert rarely leaves the mountain."

"Didn't say he wasn't on the mountain, Miss Reed."

Her gaze flicked away from him to their surroundings. The jagged rocks sloped gently here and there with stretches of somewhat level ground—much of it still covered in snow. In addition to the house, there was a small shed with a window, and an even smaller shed without one. A horse with a heavy coat was standing in the shelter of it. The cattle that were supposedly being run on the ranch were nowhere in sight. Not unusual. Reportedly, there were less than a hundred head. On thousands and thousands of acres. "You're saying he just, what?" She waved her hand. "Went out for a stroll?"

"I'm saying he's not available." He gestured toward the deck. "You want to check it out for yourself, be my guest. Meanwhile, I have things to do." He angled away from her, heading toward the back of the property from where he'd appeared in the first place. The dog lingered behind, his lip curled up again to deliver his last thoughts before finally trotting off.

She waited until both beasts had disappeared from sight, and deliberately relaxed her jaw. "Pleasant," she muttered under her breath, and closed the distance to the deck. She chewed the inside of her lip, looking underneath it, and then straightened again.

She hoped it was sounder than it looked as she gingerly went up the creaking steps. She stepped her way around the missing boards, then stopped in front of the door, knocking several times. Loudly.

There was no answer.

She exhaled and walked to the far end of the deck, where it wasn't projecting off the edge of the cliff. She looked off to the side of the house. There was no sign of man—young or old. No sign of the dog.

She tried knocking on the front door again, to no avail.

She still wasn't inclined to believe that Lambert had forgotten the appointment.

She returned to the steps and sat down on the top one, feeling relatively secure since there was at least solid earth beneath the wood, in case her rear end went through it. She dragged her briefcase onto her lap and delved inside. She pulled out her cell phone and checked it for a signal, not surprised there was none. There were still many places around Weaver where cell signals didn't yet reach. At times, like now, it was entirely frustrating. At others, when a person wanted to get entirely away from the outside world, it was an absolute delight. Remained to be seen what Gage would do about that fact.

She shook her hair out of her eyes as she slid

the phone back in its pocket and took out a business card and a pen instead.

"What's she doing out there now?"

Jed frowned, looking out one of the square, high-set windows. "Still sitting on the step." She'd been there a solid thirty minutes now. As if she were waiting for Otis to drive up the broken road. He glanced at his boss. "Next time you think twice about keeping a meeting you arranged, cancel it yourself."

Otis sucked at his teeth as he rocked in his wood-slatted rocker. For anyone else, the rocker would sit on a front porch. For Otis, it sat in front of the woodstove. No cushion for comfort. The ancient knitted blanket on his knees was a recent addition. Along with the hacking cough that was never going to go away. "I didn't expect a girl."

Jed looked out the window once more. From his angle, he could see the back of her copper-colored head and a bit of shoulder outlined in sleek black leather. If she sat there five more minutes, he was going back out there, no matter how pissed off Otis got.

"Man. Woman." Which April Reed definitely was. "Does it make any difference, Otis? We both know you're not gonna sell. Particularly to a developer." God knew they'd had enough arguments about it, especially in the last few years.

The only sound that came from Otis's direction was the rhythmic creak of wood runners on the wood floor.

Jed grimaced. "Stubborn old man."

The creaking didn't hesitate. "Keeps me alive, boy."

For how much longer?

Jed didn't ask the question. He didn't want to hear the answer. Ornery or not, Otis was the last thing left in the world that Jed cared about and he was dying. Dying because he wouldn't seek the medical care that he'd probably needed since before Jed had met him five years ago.

But he didn't have to test Otis's temper, because the redhead was moving finally. Standing.

She walked back to the door and he expected to hear a knock, but none came. Instead, after a moment she headed back to the steps, avoiding the rotten boards that Jed needed to repair once the weather finally improved. Then he caught a glimpse of her again, walking toward the road.

Tall. Slender. Dressed in a trim jacket and sexy-as-hell boots.

She looked like she belonged on a magazine cover. Or in an office cracking out orders to her minions.

Instead, she was being snubbed by a cantankerous old man.

As he watched, she slung her briefcase strap

across her chest like a messenger bag and pulled something from it.

A cell phone, he realized, watching her hold it out in front of her. She was obviously taking pictures. Maybe recording video. Her arm panned around until she was aiming it toward the cabin. He didn't worry about her seeing him from his vantage point inside.

Eventually, she panned the other direction and started making her way down the road again. When she was out of sight entirely, he went to the front door and pulled it open.

The business card she'd tucked in the doorjamb slid free and landed on the floor near his boot.

He picked it up and read the embossed black printing. It told him little more than what she'd told him outside. April Reed. Stanton Development. Denver, Colorado.

On the reverse, she'd written a telephone number and a brief note.

"She's going to be back," he told Otis. He wasn't sure if he was glad about that or not.

"How do you know?"

He flicked the business card onto Otis's lap. "She told you so."

Otis harrumphed. He looked at the note. "You can deal with her."

"She's not my problem."

"She is if I say she is." Otis smiled slyly. "That

bother you for some reason? Been a while since you've gotten off the mountain to see a woman."

"It's been a while since I've gotten off the mountain because I've been stuck up here all winter with *you*."

"All the more reason." He waved the note. "You know how to make a business deal. Or have you forgotten?"

Jed ignored the dig. "You're not going to make a deal with anyone and we both know it. I run the Rad for you, Otis. But that doesn't make me your lackey." He headed out of the room.

"Where you going?" Otis's querulous voice followed him.

"To take care of the stuff you *do* pay me for."

Chapter Two

"Well? How'd it go?"

April made a face at her friend Piper Madison and began shrugging out of her jacket as she slipped onto the barstool next to her. "It didn't."

They were at Colbys Bar & Grill, which was doing brisk business for a Thursday afternoon.

Piper looked sympathetic. "Sorry. I know you hate disappointing that sexy boss of yours."

April rolled her eyes. "That's what I get for introducing you when you came to visit."

Piper chuckled. "You're probably the only female on the planet who wouldn't be attracted to Gage Stanton. Tall, dark, rich?"

"How about demanding, a perfectionist and arrogant?"

"Sounds like someone I used to know." The pretty blonde owner of Colbys stopped in front of them on the other side of the bar. "Let me guess." Jane's smile was wry. "Talking about your boss? How is it working for Gage?"

April figured her smile was equally wry. She knew that Jane and Gage had been briefly married ages ago, before Jane had moved to Weaver. Long before she'd married April's cousin Casey Clay. "Never dull, that's for sure."

Jane chuckled. "So, what can I get you?"

"Just some coffee to start." Deciding she was too chilly, she pulled her jacket back on. "What's the special for lunch today?"

"Chicken enchiladas."

"They're good, too. Had them last week," Piper offered. She already had a salad in front of her that she'd partially consumed.

"Enchiladas it is," April told Jane. "How's life with my cousin and those babies?" Casey and Jane had recently adopted twins.

Jane winked as she keyed in the order. "Never dull, that's for sure." She turned up a mug in front of April and filled it with coffee. She wiped the gleaming wood bar top with her towel. "Piper, you need a refill?"

"Not yet." Piper waited until Jane had moved

down the bar again before she spoke. "I completely forget that Jane was ever married to Gage. Criminy. Where's the fairness in life? I can't get a date, and she has had not one hottie hubby, but two."

"You most certainly *can* get a date," April chided.

"Sure, if I lived somewhere other than Weaver," Piper complained. "Here, I'll forever be just the preacher's kid who teaches sixth grade."

"Then move to Denver," April said immediately. "You can split the ridiculous rent on my apartment with me."

"Much as I love that fancy loft of yours, you know I can't."

"I know you won't," April countered without heat. "So stop complaining. If I've said it once, I've said it a hundred times. If there is someone you want to date, ask *him*. You don't have to wait around waiting to be asked."

"Too bad all women don't have your confidence. You've always had guys falling at your feet, too. Maybe it's the fact that you're tall, svelte and red-headed while I am a short, round and forgettable brownette."

April couldn't help but laugh. "You exaggerate more than anyone I've ever known." She was tall, but keeping from looking like a living scarecrow was as much a problem for her as Piper's lifelong battle against the fifteen extra pounds she didn't want.

Her friend's eyes were twinkling. "It's not an

exaggeration when it comes to Mr. Perfect Financial Planner."

April sighed faintly and stirred milk into her coffee. "Kenneth was fun, but—"

"He made the ultimate mistake. He got serious and you didn't."

"Unlike you, I'm not interested in settling down yet." She started to lift her coffee, but set it down again. "Who proposes to a woman they've only been dating a few months? We never even slept together." Exasperation suddenly churned inside her because she knew she'd hurt Kenneth, no matter how unintentionally. "I mean, really. Who would take a proposal like that seriously?"

Unfazed by April's waving hands, Piper pushed her salad to the side and scooped up a blob of guacamole with a tortilla chip. "All the people who've fallen in love at first sight? Maybe Kenneth's just the old-fashioned type." She popped the chip in her mouth and crunched on it.

"No man I've ever met is that old-fashioned." April exhaled. Piper might lament her romantic vacuum, but on a daily basis, she successfully corralled a roomful of hormonal preadolescents. What was one agitated redhead? Piper's equanimity was soothing.

"Well, I forever live in hope that there are a few old-fashioned guys still out there," Piper said wryly. She took another scoop of guacamole, this time eschewing the chip and going straight at it with the tip of her fork. "But back to your meeting. What do you mean, *it didn't?*"

"I mean I never even had a chance to see Otis Lambert." Jed Dalloway's face swam inside April's head. She shivered and not even wrapping her hands around the hot coffee mug helped. "Did you know the road up to his place is blocked off? Probably a half mile back from the house. There was obviously a rockslide at some point. Huge boulders on the road. The wood barricades look like they've been there awhile."

"Since there's never been any reason for me *to* drive up there, no, I didn't know. So when he set the meeting, he didn't mention it."

"Nope." She stretched out one leg. "Had to walk the rest of the way in these."

"You've routinely worn four-inch heels since you earned your first paycheck. You expect sympathy?"

April grinned. "Obviously not from you."

"So, you hoofed it in high heels and then what?"

"And then nothing. He wasn't there. At least that's what I was told."

"By whom?"

"Jed Dalloway." She eyed her friend. Except when they'd spent four years as college roommates, Piper had lived her entire life in Weaver. "Have you met him?"

"Not that I recall. I've heard his name, of course,

but unless he has kids in school, not much reason I would have."

"He didn't exactly strike me as the family type."

Piper chuckled. "Why? Wasn't he wearing his sign?"

"Ha ha." She looked down at her coffee, seeing instead Jed's dark eyes. "Otis Lambert doesn't need to post No Trespass signs. All he has to do is post Jed Dalloway on the road."

"Off-putting, I take it."

"His attitude is." She shook her head, as if to rid him from her thoughts. "I left my card. Said I'd be back." She was briefly interrupted when a server delivered her meal. She thanked the teenager, and began unfolding her napkin. "Why did you say of course you've heard his name?"

"Jed Dalloway's name?" Piper shrugged. "You know this town. Everyone hears about everyone, sooner or later. You want that black olive?" She was reaching even before April shook her head and Piper popped it in her mouth. "Ooh, hot." She chewed quickly, gingerly. "Heard he's from Chicago or thereabouts. Some scandal involved. So they say."

"*They* being the grapes on Weaver's prolific vine?"

"You know it." Piper dashed her fingertips with her napkin. Her smile was mischievous. "Not that *I* listen to gossip."

April's lips twitched. "Of course not." She cut into her steaming enchiladas. "So what *is* the good gossip around town?"

"As usual, half of it involves members of your family. You think I'm going to say?"

April laughed. "Now I know you're exaggerating."

Piper chuckled. "Maybe a little." She glanced at her watch. "I have fifteen minutes before I need to be back at school for a teachers meeting. Pick a category." She held up her hand. "Money problems? Marital discord?" She ticked them off on her fingers. "Politics? Sex scandals?"

"Oh for Pete's sake. Sex scandals?"

"Just because we're small town, doesn't mean we're not keeping up with the Joneses. There's a rumor that Vivian Templeton is paying for more than architectural designs when it comes to the new town library she's trying to get built."

April rolled her eyes. Vivian Templeton was the sister-in-law of Squire Clay's deceased first wife. Even though she'd never met the woman herself, she knew Vivian had to be well in her eighties. Maybe more. April wasn't related to her, but her mom's stepbrothers were. Which meant the wealthy eccentric was family of a sort. "I have a hard time imagining it, but Vivian's first husband made his fortune in steel. Supposedly she can afford whatever she wants to spend her money on, so if she's not hurting anyone, who cares? I mean other than

Squire." Her grandfather held a grudge against Vivian over a supposed insult to his first wife.

Piper shrugged. "Beck's firm is handling the design."

That *was* news. "People think Beck would cha-cha with an elderly rich lady when he has my cousin at home? Talk about ridiculous."

"He's not the only architect at his firm."

"Yeah, there's Nick," she said dismissively. "Can't see that one, either." Nick was Beck's son from his first marriage. "He's two years younger than me."

Piper spread her hands. "I'm just the messenger. So, what's your plan with Mr. Lambert?"

"I'll go back tomorrow. And the next day. And the next if I have to."

"That would be Sunday. Easter Sunday."

April made a face. "Okay, maybe not Easter Sunday."

"How long're you planning to be in town?"

"Depends on how things go. I'm meeting with Archer Templeton next Tuesday." The attorney practiced in Colorado and Wyoming and, among other things, represented Stanton Development in both states. "He's doing research on possible claims that might arise against the Rambling Rad."

Piper rolled her eyes. "Another hottie. Man, you do get all the luck."

April made a face. "Archer's cut from the same cloth as my boss. Not my type. At all."

"Do you even know what your type is?"

Once again, Jed's face flitted through her mind. Strong legs braced and short dark hair whipping in the wind.

Fortunately, Piper was pulling out her wallet and didn't seem to think anything about April's lack of an answer. "Just stay long enough that we can get together again before you leave."

"I will. And put your money away. I told you I'd get lunch."

"Just because you earn three times as much as I do and have a trust fund the size of Alaska doesn't mean I can't buy my own lunch."

"That's true." April plucked the wallet out of her friend's hands and zipped it shut again. "But I've got per diem expense money to use up one way or another and staying at the big house means either buying you a bunch of lunches or going shopping. I'll never use up the funds otherwise."

Piper grinned. "Life is really rough working for that sexy developer of yours." She put away her wallet and slid off the barstool. She gave April a quick hug and gathered up her belongings before sending a wave toward Jane as she pulled on her coat and left.

When her friend was gone, April turned back to her sufficiently cooled enchiladas. When she finished eating, she pushed the plate aside and pulled out her phone, studying the photographs she'd taken up on the mountain. She discarded a few, forwarded the rest to her boss and continued reviewing the emails she'd received.

She'd only gotten through two when her phone vibrated. She swiped the screen and held it to her ear. "That was fast."

"Landslide." Gage's tone was typically brief and to the point. "Happen often?"

"I have no idea," she admitted. "I'll find out, though." She could see Jane from the corner of her eye, pulling drinks at the other end of the bar and wondered, not for the first time, if Gage's ex-wife was one more reason why he hadn't come to Weaver himself. Jane was now a happily married woman with a family. Gage—for all of his eligible bachelor reputation—had always struck April as distinctly lonely.

"Let me know." On that, he ended the call in his typically abrupt way and she went back to answering her emails. Two cups of coffee later, she'd finished. She paid the bill and headed out.

The clouds had blown away. The sky was a bright blue, the air brittle and cold even through her leather jacket. She debated driving back up the mountain to see if Lambert had suddenly become "available," but decided against it. In the note she'd left, she said she'd return the next day. Whether or not Otis Lambert stood by his words, she would stand by hers. Ambushing a man who was ill just wasn't her style.

She drove to the far side of town, where Shop-World was located and where she knew the cell signal was the strongest of anywhere in town. She found an available parking spot in a sunny corner and pulled out her laptop. Even though she knew the contents of the Rambling project file backward and forward, she read through it again while she called the State Geological Survey. The woman on the phone told her that Lambert had made no report of the landslide. Strictly speaking, he didn't have to. The only thing that appeared to have been impacted had been the road. His private road.

Nevertheless, she retrieved all the history she could of geological events that had occurred in the area and sent the information in a summarized email to her boss.

By the time she finished, she was colder than ever from sitting in her idle car and the bright lights of Shop-World were beckoning. She put away her computer and grabbed her wallet and headed toward the busy supersized store. She went first to the clothing department and found an inexpensive, insulated coat. She added a knit scarf with a matching beanie and gloves to her armload, and then swung by the grocery department to grab some chocolate, because—well, there never needed to be a specific reason for chocolate.

Her phone buzzed and she juggled her armload as she pulled it from the pocket of her jacket. Another message from her boss. While Gage was unfailingly brief verbally, the same couldn't be said when it came to his texts and email messages.

Reading through his latest, she headed toward the registers at the front of the store only to bump right into a pyramid of paper towels. She cursed under her breath, dropping the coat and scarf and trying to keep the entire display from toppling. She managed, but several rolls escaped her, and she chased after them, snatching them up.

"...*and* that's why I keep telling you to watch where you're going," she heard a woman say as a noisy cart rumbled past her.

"And that's why we should keep our noses out of our phones," April mumbled after her, meeting the little boy's eyes as he trotted after his mama. He smiled at her and she couldn't help smile back as she stuffed one roll after another back onto the now-lopsided pyramid.

"You missed one."

She looked up, first at the extended roll of towels. Then the long, square-tipped fingers grasping it. The masculine wrist beyond. Her stomach was sinking even before she got to his face.

She grabbed her items and straightened from her

graceless crouch, taking the roll from him to set on the pile. Brown, she realized. His eyes were a deep dark, chocolate brown. "Mr. Dalloway."

And there was definitely a bite of amusement in those eyes, even though it didn't translate to any other part of his face. Maybe he wasn't handsome in a conventional sense. But he was definitely arresting.

"Miss Reed." He turned on his boot heel and started to walk away.

She renewed her grip on her items and followed. "I left my card for your boss," she said to his back. She was purchasing a cheap coat. He only wore the same clothes he'd worn earlier that day as if he were impervious to the cold weather. "I told him I'd be returning tomorrow."

His shoulders moved impatiently and he stopped to look at her. Lines radiated from the corners of his eyes, and she could tell he spent a lot of time squinting in the sun. She had a dozen relatives who possessed those exact same kind of lines.

But what put the lines around his tightly held lips?

"Another day's not going to matter," he was saying. "He's not going to see you tomorrow. Or any other day. He's not selling. And definitely not to a developer."

He wasn't saying anything that her grandfather hadn't already said. She wanted to believe Jed as little as she wanted to believe Squire. "Then why'd he ask to meet with Stanton Development?"

"Why does Otis do any of the things he does?" He spread his hands and she noticed then the small brown prescription bottle he held. "Not even sure Otis himself knows."

"You, ah, you run the ranch for him, don't you? The Rambling Rad. Are you afraid of losing your job?"

His lips twisted. "He's not going to sell, Miss Reed. My involvement with the ranch, such as it is, is as immaterial to him as it is to you."

"It's not immaterial! I assure you, the company I work for isn't about putting people *out* of work. It's about creating *more* opportunities!"

His expression didn't change. She couldn't tell if he believed her or not. "My advice would be to go back to Colorado. Focus your efforts on greener pastures." He turned to go again.

"I'm sorry that he's ill, Mr. Dalloway."

He didn't look back. "So am I, Miss Reed."

She chewed the inside of her cheek, watching him step around a Shop-World employee stocking a shelf with Easter candy. He was aiming for the pharmacy.

If she were really a bloodthirsty developer, she'd race for her car to get up the mountain for a chance to get to Otis before Jed could.

Instead, she joined the lines at the registers, paid for her items and drove back out to the big house.

By the time she let herself in through the back door, it was nearly dark outside and the smell of home cooking was heady.

Everyone was already seated around the kitchen table and she dumped off her briefcase and purchases in the mudroom before washing her hands and joining them. "Sorry I'm late." She slipped into the empty chair next to her grandmother.

"Don't be silly." Gloria handed her a steaming platter piled high with roasted vegetables and beef. "We just sat down anyway."

April took the platter and scooped a helping onto her plate. Despite the lunch at Colbys, her stomach was already growling. "Smells wonderful." She passed it on to Matthew, who was at the head of the table. "At the rate I'm eating, I won't fit in my clothes by the time I go back to Denver."

Squire snorted. He was at the other end of the table. "Too thin as it is. Could stand some meat on your bones. Just like your mama."

Gloria tsked. "Leave her alone."

April didn't bother hiding her smile as her grandfather harrumphed. Squire Clay might have the sternest face imaginable, but he was a complete softie where his grandchildren and great-grandchildren were concerned. Whether they were grown like April, or still young, he was guaranteed to be their biggest partner in crime. Which was pretty sweet, considering the stories April had grown up with about what a hard-ass he'd been as a father.

"I thought I'd go see Aunt Belle soon," she told Gloria. "If you want to come?" Belle and April's mother, Nikki, were twins. "I'll see if Lucy can join us, too." Lucy was Belle's stepdaughter.

"It's a plan." Gloria smiled.

Eventually, talk turned to ranch business, and April let it wash over her as she worked her way through her food.

"How'd things go up on the mountain?"

The question was inevitable, of course. She gave her grandfather a grimace. "Like you expected."

"Sorry to be right, girl."

"No you're not," Matthew scoffed, giving April a wink. "You love being right."

"When I'm dealing with sons who don't know their heads from a hole in the ground," Squire shot back without heat.

"Regardless, I'm not giving up," April assured them.

"Damn straight," Squire said, nodding approvingly. "This family never gives up."

"True," Gloria said brightly, giving her husband a deliberate look. "Which is why I've sent in our RSVP for the fund-raiser." She extended a basket of golden rolls toward him. "*Two* will be attending."

His brows pulled down. He ignored the basket. "I told you we were *not* going to that thing."

The hand holding the basket didn't move an inch. "And I told you that we were."

His lips thinned.

There had always been plenty of standoffs between her grandparents so April knew better than to worry as the tension between them thickened. "What's the fund-raiser for?"

"New library," Jaimie said. "Vivian's latest project. She's hosting a big do at her home. Has invited half the state, from what I hear."

Understanding hit. Squire detested anything related to Vivian Templeton. And he considered the lavish home that she'd built to be an eyesore. "Building a new library is a good thing, though."

"And long past due," Gloria said in agreement. "The one we have occupies that small two-story down by the town square and it's nowhere near large enough anymore to serve the entire town. Enlarging the present location isn't feasible, so that means finding a way to build a new one." She was still giving her husband a stern eye and the basket of rolls was still extended. "Regardless of who is spearheading the effort."

He grimaced. "Doesn't mean I am going to go out to her house and pretend we're all friends." He snatched away the basket, grabbed a roll and pointed it at Matthew. "That woman shunned your mama," he reminded before slapping the roll down on his plate.

"Before we were born," Matthew said mildly.

"S'pose that means *you're* going, too?" Squire looked even more annoyed.

"Squire, Vivian has made some significant contributions in the few years since she moved here," Jaimie tried in a pacifying tone. "The new hospital wing, the—"

"People like her can always throw money at a cause," he cut her off. "Thinking it covers up what they're really like."

"Vivian isn't trying to cover up anything," Gloria said wearily. "She's been perfectly honest about regretting the things she's said and done in the past. She's apologized. You're the one who won't accept it. And if you won't go with your own wife to the fund-raiser, I'll find someone who will." She pushed away from the table and stomped out of the room.

Squire cursed under his breath and stomped out of the room, too. A second later, they heard the back door slam as he left the house.

Standoffs between her grandparents were normal. Walking away in opposite directions was not.

Alarm gurgling inside her, April looked from her aunt's face to her uncle's. "Should we go after them?"

"Not if you want to keep your head attached to your body," Matthew advised.

Jaimie got up and began clearing the dishes. "They'll be fine," she soothed. "Squire must feel like he's on the losing end of the battle where everyone's acceptance of Vivian is concerned. You know him. That just isn't going to sit well."

April handed Jaimie the roll basket. "Was what she did really so bad?"

"You know what Squire is like when it comes to family," Matthew said. "When her husband found out that my mom was his illegitimate half sister, Vivian lost it. Those were the days when anyone illegitimate was treated like a pariah, but her husband was all set to bring my mother into the family fold anyway. He died in a car accident before he had a chance to actually do that. Evidently there were rumors it was suicide."

"Which Vivian categorically denies." Jaimie slid her hand over Matthew's shoulder. "And your mother died when she had Tristan around that same time. One of those weird tragic coincidences."

"I can still remember Squire coming home from the hospital with Tris wrapped in a blanket. Alone." Matthew shook his head and brushed an absent kiss over Jaimie's knuckles. "Who knows what kind of relationship they might have had if they'd lived."

"Even though their marriage was far from perfect, Vivian says her husband loved their sons too much to leave them deliberately," Jaimie told April.

"In any case, Squire's never likely to forgive Vivian for treating my mother the way she did." Matthew rose with his plate in hand.

Jaimie spoke gently. "I think Vivian's contributions around Weaver—the money she's investing—is a way of atoning for that. She's going to do what she's going to do regardless of what anyone—particularly Squire—thinks about it. Since he was elected to the town council, he hasn't been able to avoid her as much as he'd like to."

"He seems to be going to great lengths to avoid her," said April.

"Don't worry about him and your grandma," Matthew advised. "The old man doesn't have a lot of things these days to be obstreperous about, so when he has a chance, he really goes at it. He'll come around if only to appease Gloria."

"He can save his appeasing," Gloria said, sailing into the kitchen in time to overhear. "That coot of mine can just stay home. April will be my date for the fund-raiser, won't you, dear?"

"When is it?"

"Week from Saturday."

She chewed the inside of her cheek. "I'd be happy to, but I'm not sure I'll be here that long. Depends how things go with Mr. Lambert."

"Well, I want you to succeed, of course," Gloria said, "but anything that keeps you here with us a little bit longer is just fine with me. Next time you go up the mountain to see Otis, take a covered dish.

Have never known two men living on their own to turn down a pretty girl bearing home-cooked food."

April groaned. "Grandma, that is so old-fashioned."

"Maybe so." Gloria nodded sagely. "But I'll bet you it works."

Chapter Three

The next afternoon, April—wearing her new coat and scarf and gloves—went up the mountain again. She was not resorting to her grandmother's suggestion of taking a covered dish. She wasn't meeting Lambert for a church potluck dinner, for heaven's sake.

But once again, she went back down the mountain after an hour, having failed to get past the front door of that miserable little shack. Like the first time, she spent the rest of the day with her computer and her phone, gathering more research and reporting it all back to Gage.

That evening, when she got together with some of her cousins at Colbys, she had to recount the effort to meet Lambert yet again. "The only bright spot, if I can call it that," she said over the hot cider she was drinking, "was that Jed Dalloway wasn't around this time to witness my failure."

"It's not a failure," Lucy assured. She was sitting across the tables they'd shoved together to accommodate the number of cousins who kept showing up. "Unless you're giving up already."

"Squire would kick me out from under his roof if I were." April pulled a crispy French fry from the enormous mound in the center of the tables and dredged it in ketchup. "Not to mention my boss would probably give me the boot, too." She wasn't really worried about that, but neither did she want to return to Colorado with nothing to show for it. Not on the very first assignment she'd been charged with heading. She wouldn't exactly blame Gage if he didn't repeat the mistake any time soon.

"I'm sure that wouldn't happen." That came from Sarah, who was Matthew and Jaimie's daughter and taught at the same school as Piper. She kept casting an eye toward the pool tables where her nineteen-year-old daughter, Megan, was playing with friends. "You know the worst part about kids turning nineteen?" She jabbed her French fry in the air. "You lose your ability to ground them when they keep doing dumb things."

April looked over toward the group in question. Despite the cold weather, Megan wore a pair of denim shorts, cowboy boots and a skintight T-shirt. She was blonde and impossibly lovely in the way that only nineteen-year-old girls could be. "What kind of dumb things?"

"The usual. Staying out too late. Hanging with the wrong crowd."

"How does the sheriff's daughter manage to hang out with the wrong crowd?"

"Probably because she *is* the sheriff's daughter." The suggestion came from their cousin Courtney as she slipped into a free chair. "Trust one who knows."

"Don't worry so much about Megan," Lucy soothed. "All of us around that age tested the boundaries. We've all come out on the other side more or less intact. And her brother has a good head on his shoulders. Megan always listens to him."

April felt the whoosh of cold air when the door started to open and she glanced over, half expecting to see another one of her cousins arriving.

But the man who entered was no relative of hers.

And for whatever reason, Jed Dalloway's focus seemed to land right on her face when he let the door swing closed behind him.

She felt a rush of heat in her face and quickly looked away, which only made her feel stupid. For all of Vivian Templeton's fancy fund-raisers for new libraries and such, Weaver was still a small town. Running into familiar faces in public establishments was commonplace.

A bright peal of laughter rose above the general noise of voices and jukebox music, and April glanced toward the pool tables to see Megan leaning against a young man, laughing merrily. He slid his hand down Megan's backside. April grimaced and looked away, glad that Sarah hadn't seen.

In truth, at twenty-eight, April was as close to Megan's age as she was to Sarah's. She felt for both mother and daughter.

"So what's everyone wearing to the library fundraiser?" The question came from Courtney. "I don't think my closetful of scrubs will quite cut it at a Vivian Templeton production."

The topic made April think about her grandparents. Squire and Gloria still hadn't been speaking that morning at breakfast. "It's not a formal affair, is it?" She couldn't imagine how such a thing would be particularly successful in Weaver, where a lot of folks' idea of dressing up meant washing the mud off their boots and pressing a crease into the legs of their blue jeans.

"Cocktail attire," Courtney answered, "according to the invitation."

"In other words, wear a couple sequins with the jeans," Jane suggested dryly. "I know Vivian pretty well by now. She might seem like an eccentric snob at times, but she's a lot less uptight about that sort of thing than appears. And she knows people will kick in money for her library project if only for the chance to see inside her mansion." She looked around her and muttered something under her breath as she pushed to her feet and began clearing the empties from a nearby table to carry back to the bar.

Jed had taken one of the few empty barstools and despite her best efforts, April's attention kept sliding to him. He was facing away from her, which didn't help any. It only meant some kernel of her mind decided it was okay to study him, free from discovery.

A ridiculous notion, of course. The man could look up at any moment and see what was going on behind him courtesy of the long mirror hanging on the wall behind the bar.

Nevertheless, she continued to study him.

The wide shoulders, bowed a little. A result of the arms he'd propped on the gleaming wooden bar top? Or the weight of working for a man like Otis?

She looked down at her hands, more than a little oblivious to the conversations flowing around her.

She wasn't aware of any plan to stand until she found herself on her feet. But there she was, skirting tables and making her way to the bar.

She angled between Jed and the person occupying the barstool next to him. "Buy you a drink?" It came out more breathless than she intended.

He didn't look up at her, but looked up to face the mirror instead, catching her gaze in the reflection there. "I don't drink."

She couldn't help the way her eyebrows rose a little. He had a squat glass sitting in front of him, half-filled with amber liquid, and when she lifted it and sniffed, she knew it was scotch. "Okay." She set the glass precisely where it had been. "Buy you a coffee, instead?"

He finally shifted, looking at her straight on with those dark, chocolate eyes.

For no reason whatsoever, her mouth suddenly felt dry.

"You won't get to Otis through me."

"Sometimes the offer of a coffee is just a coffee, Jed."

"What happened to Mr. Dalloway?"

She glanced around the bar. "I don't know." The woman on the barstool beside him shifted, forcing April to shift, as well. Her shoulder brushed accidentally against Jed's before she managed to scoot back a few inches. "It's Friday night. The mister and miss stuff can come back out on Monday morning."

His lips actually stretched into a semblance of a smile. Just enough to make something unfamiliar inside her flitter around.

He turned slightly, and his thigh brushed against her leg. Only *he* didn't scoot back.

"The gesture's appreciated," he finally said.

"Miss Reed." He twisted on the barstool again. No longer touching.

That flittering fizzled and sank.

She managed a smile but could see by her own reflection in the mirror that it looked just as tight as it felt.

She looked down at his seemingly untouched glass of whisky. "Enjoy your—" she turned her palm upward "—whatever, then. Jed."

She skirted the crowd that had been thickening and returned to her seat only to find that three more relatives had joined their group.

She pushed cheerfulness into her voice. "Definitely turning out to be ladies' night," she said as she sat back down after exchanging quick hugs with them all.

"Hey." Nick, Lucy's stepson, tossed a balled-up napkin toward her. "What about me? I pee standing up."

April grinned, managing to push off the worst of her Jed-lag. "Charming as always, Nick."

He flashed a dimple and tilted his bottle of beer in her direction.

She leaned toward him. Of all of her cousins, he was the closest to her in age. "Rumor has it you're romancing Weaver's newest billionaire widow."

He looked only vaguely chagrined. "Vivian Templeton is too much for any sane man to take on. Young or old."

She laughed. "Congratulations, though. I hear you're working on the big library project."

He nodded. "I had to promise Dad the moon for him to give it to me. After working with her for the past few months, I'd steal the moon just to give the project back to him."

"She's that hard to work with?"

"Let's just say she's…different." He held up his palms. "She wants the Taj Mahal. Has me work up something." His right hand dipped and his left rose like a scale. "Then practicality strikes. Has me changing it all again. Back and forth. Up and down. Every time we meet. Extravagance one day. Then the next it's 'Dear Arthur' and she backtracks all over hell and back again."

"Ah, *Dear Arthur*." Jane had returned with another tray of drinks.

April lifted her brows. "Who is Arthur?"

"Vivian's last husband and according to her, the great love of her life. Unlike all the rest of her husbands, he was a regular guy. Didn't have money, and evidently being with him taught Vivian the error of her ways. Since he died, she's been trying to right all the wrongs of her life. I think she's afraid if she doesn't she won't be joining him."

April frowned. "Morbid."

"Not from Vivian's perspective. Until Arthur, she had all the money in the world, but little happiness. She's outlived all four of her husbands. The oldest of her sons died when he was a young man. She's been estranged from her other two since they were old enough to get away, and she's spent the last several years trying to restore a relationship with them. Not having much success, I'm afraid. All of her grandchildren get on with her, but her own sons still don't want anything to do with her."

So Squire wasn't the only one who wasn't in a forgiving mood when it came to Vivian. "She sounds…interesting."

Jane chuckled. "I think she's pretty entertaining, actually. She's trying to be a better person. Personally, I think that's something to admire."

"You don't have to work with her," Nick said with feeling.

"Hey." Megan had left the pool tables momentarily. "What time is Easter dinner over at Uncle Jefferson's?"

"Two o'clock." The answer was more a chorus of responses. The whole family was going to be there.

Megan huffed. "Why couldn't they just do it right after church? It's gonna take up the whole day."

"It's Easter," Sarah reminded evenly. "It's a time for family." Her gaze traveled past her daughter. "Your new friends can wait."

The young woman rolled her eyes and turned on her heel, sashaying back to the pool tables.

Sarah sighed noisily.

"April, I imagine Kenneth will be happy when

you get back to Denver." That was from Lucy in an obvious attempt to change the focus.

"Don't think so," she answered absently. Jed had moved away from the bar and was making his way around the tables. And that flittering inside her reappeared. "He was getting too serious for me. We broke up a few weeks ago." Her eyes caught on Jed's face but he did nothing more than glance her way as he passed right by, going out the exit.

"Know him?"

April looked from the door swinging closed to Jane. "Sorry?"

"Do you know Jed?"

"Do you?"

"He comes in now and then. More often this time of year. You know how the winter gets to people."

April waited, sure there was more. "And?"

Jane shrugged. "And nothing. He lives up on the Rambling. Know he isn't a drinker. Orders a double. Doesn't drink a drop. That's about it. He's not very talkative."

"I heard he's from Chicago," someone offered.

"Thought it was Atlanta," someone else said.

"It doesn't matter to me where he comes from," April said. She looked beyond Nick's shoulder toward the exit. "As long as he doesn't get in my way."

"What does my beloved ex plan to do with the mountain if he succeeds?"

April lifted her hands. "You know Gage. Make use of as much of the mountain as he can."

"Well, at least we can trust him to be responsible with it," Jane said.

"If he gets it," April cautioned. "Right now, it's not exactly looking likely. I've tried twice to meet with Mr. Lambert and haven't managed it yet. Parked myself right on his front porch for an hour this afternoon but he never answered the door."

"He's a stubborn one all right," Courtney said.

Surprised, April looked down the table. "You've met him?"

Courtney nodded. "Once." But she didn't say anything more. April could only assume it had something to do with the old man's health. Her cousin was a nurse at the hospital, after all.

"So what happened with Kenneth?"

April looked at Nick. It was absurdly difficult pulling her thoughts away from Jed and Otis. "Kenneth? Right. Yeah. He proposed. We broke up." She suddenly pushed out of her chair. "I'll be back."

She grabbed her jacket and hurried out the door. It was already dark outside but the old-fashioned lampposts lining Main gave enough light to see along the street. She didn't see Jed, though. Not when she walked to the end of the building. Then back again.

Disappointed, she sank down on the iron bench outside of the grill and slowly pulled on her jacket.

She exhaled deeply and stretched out her legs, crossing her boots at the ankle. From inside the bar behind her, she could hear the faint pulse of country music. From the dusty pickup truck driving slowly down the street, she could hear the louder pulse of classic rock. She looked in the opposite direction and could see the mountainous peak of the Rambling, a dark shadow against the sky.

"What are you really doing up there, Otis? Is it just a mistake? Or some game you're playing?"

"It's no game."

She jerked, sitting upright. "Jed. Where'd you come from?"

He jerked his thumb and she looked across the street.

"The park?"

"Is that surprising for some reason?"

She pressed her lips together. Shook her head while she curled her fingers around the cold metal seat beneath her. "It's a nice park. The town square," she finally said. "I had my first kiss under the gazebo in the park when I was thirteen."

His only response was to tuck the tips of his fingers in the front pockets of his jeans.

She let out a breath, feeling idiotic. "I don't know why I said that."

"Is it true?"

"Yes."

"Who was the kisser?"

"Just a boy."

"Kenneth?"

She gaped. "Your hearing must be very good."

His lips compressed and he looked across the street toward the park and the gazebo that was a shadowy monolith in its own smaller way. "First girl I kissed was named Tanya."

The name itself wasn't what shocked her. The fact that he'd offered the information at all was.

She moistened her lips. "Um…his name was Scotty. Scott. He was a friend from summer camp."

"And Kenneth?"

She narrowed her eyes, studying his face. His eyebrows were dark and level. The equally dark eyes were impossible to read. He had a small white scar near the corner of his unsmiling mouth. And as usual, he seemed impervious to the cold air, wearing merely a long-sleeved T-shirt with his jeans while everyone else wore jackets and thick sweaters.

"That's actually none of your business," she finally said. "Are you impervious to the cold? It's freezing out here."

"It'll get colder. Storm is coming."

"That's not an answer."

He shrugged.

She exhaled, struggling against impatience. "Is the reason your boss hasn't met with me because he's too sick? Frail?"

"That's actually none of *your* business."

"A deal with Stanton might help him."

Jed just looked at her and she felt that weird fluttering start up again. "You know," she added hurriedly. "We're talking significant money. That goes a long way for treatments. Or medicine. Whatever he needs."

"You think he doesn't know that?"

She swallowed and rubbed her palms down the front of her jeans as she rose. Remaining seated while he stood was just too much of a disadvantage. "I don't know what he knows, do I? Having not had an opportunity to actually speak with him." She crossed her arms and eyed him suspiciously. "Are you preventing him from having visitors?"

He gave a snort that sounded genuinely amused. "You seem to be under the delusion that I can control anything where Otis is concerned. The man does what he wants, Miss Reed."

She spread her arms. "Oh, come on. It's still Friday evening. Can't we dispense with that? I mean, you know my romantic history now," she said lightly. "I know yours."

His dark eyes seemed to go even darker. "No." He pulled his fingers from his pockets. "You don't." He started to walk away but stopped after a few feet. "Come tomorrow around three." His voice was low. Gruff. "I'll see what I can do."

She nodded, because she was too surprised to actually get out a word.

Then, he was gone, disappearing around the corner of Colbys.

She ought to feel some sense of success. But all she felt was bewildered.

"Hey, April." Nick stuck his head out of the door. "You all right?"

She nodded. "Needed some fresh air."

He looked concerned. "You rushed out after I mentioned Kenneth." He made a face. "And all that. I didn't mean to upset you."

"I'm not upset."

He was obviously unconvinced. "You're sure?"

She tucked her arm through his. "Honestly."

"Then come back in. I'm feeling outnumbered by females."

"You know, I *am* a female, too."

"Eh." Nick made a face. "I s'pose."

"Like I said. Charming as ever, Nick."

"That's me. Nick Charming."

She laughed and headed back into the warm, bustling bar, determined to leave thoughts of Jed Not-Charming out in the cold where he belonged.

Chapter Four

"She won't come," Otis said. "Rain's on the way. Only fools would drive up in the rain."

Jed stirred up sparks in the woodstove and tossed in another log. He shut the door and adjusted the air intake to make sure the flame took. Just because he always ran hot, didn't mean Otis did, and the woodstove was the only source of heat in the cabin.

"Sick o' winter," he muttered, straightening from his crouch.

Otis laughed, though it was at least 70 percent cough. "You picked a bad place to live then," he wheezed. "In a place where winter can use up three of the four seasons."

"Didn't pick Wyoming." He shoved his fingers

through his hair and rolled up his sleeves as he moved to the window. "Picked me, if you remember." More accurately, Otis had picked him.

Literally off the floor of a bar in Texas. Out of the bottle and the drugs. Away from anything and everything that Jed had used to forget the past. To forget everything and everyone he'd lost.

If it weren't for Otis, Jed would probably be dead. Or still wishing he were.

He still kept the past at bay. Now he just did it working a small herd of cattle on the side of a mountain, where one misstep could be the difference between life and death.

The thick clouds hanging around the mountain obscured the view of the town far below. Visibility driving up there would be particularly bad.

He'd told her to come at three because that was usually the time that Otis was awake between naps. When he'd have enough energy and appetite to swallow down some stew or, if it was a really good day, some eggs or even a few bites of steak.

It was only two o'clock now. He hoped to hell the redhead had the good sense not to come up the mountain. Not in this weather.

He looked over at Otis. He doubted the man had ever been built like a bear. More like a wily fox. In the five years since Jed had been with him, the fox had withered. Weakened.

The wily, though?

Jed wasn't putting any bets on that trait diminishing at all.

"What did you do with that business card she left the other day?"

"Tossed it."

Jed gave him a look.

Otis rubbed his hand over the sparse white whiskers sprouting unevenly over his bony jaw. "Don't recall."

He raised his eyebrow.

The old man sighed noisily. He lifted one of the library books that Jed kept him supplied with and pulled the card from inside the pages.

Jed took it and went into the kitchen. There was one phone on the mountain and it was straight out of another era. Heavy black plastic with a rotary dial and a long curly cord.

He dialed the number that April had written on the back of the business card, but the line went straight to voice mail. Common occurrence when it came to calling cell phones. Even more so when there was a storm brewing.

He didn't figure the message would ever be received, but he left one anyway. "Stay off the road in the rain."

He turned down the heat under the venison stew he'd picked up the night before from Bubba Bumble down in Weaver. The guy was a short order cook at Ruby's Diner, but he kept Jed supplied with home-cooked meals for Otis. Jed could manage scrambled eggs and standard meat and potatoes, but not anything much fancier. The few times he'd tried over the years had not been successes. It was a lot easier to go to a source who knew what he was doing.

Jed had hoped the stew—something Otis used to want routinely—would be a temptation now for Otis's dwindling appetite.

He left the card sitting on the counter next to the phone and went back into the other room. Otis was slumped in his chair, book open on his lap, but his eyes were closed. Snoring slightly.

He was sleeping more and more.

Jed moved the book to the table by the chair and Otis didn't stir. The fire was burning well so he adjusted the intake, then snapped his fingers at the dog.

Samson uncurled and shook himself, then followed Jed out of the room and back into the kitchen. Aside from the kitchen and living area, there was a single bathroom and a single bedroom and the entirety of the whole place could have fit into the master bedroom that Jed once shared with Tanya.

He knew why she kept sneaking into his thoughts.

It was like that every spring. After eight years, the memories ought to have dulled. After eight years, he'd given up thinking that they would.

Samson followed him out the back door and his ears perked up. The shepherd mix took off running, but Jed didn't worry about him. The dog had been with Otis longer than Jed had.

He crossed to the shack that had been his home ever since Otis had come into his life. Otis told him it had originally been a potting shed for his mother. Apparently the concession on his father's part hadn't been enough to tempt her to stay on the mountain, where life was just too damn hard.

Until Jed came along, the structure had mostly been used to shelter calves when necessary.

Jed had shared the space with more than one orphaned calf in the years he'd been there. But he'd made a few changes.

He had a bed on one side of the room. An efficiency kitchen on the other, where the potting bench had once stood. The bathroom was in one closet, his clothes in the other. His only indulgence where modern technology was concerned was the radio that ran under any circumstances. If the electricity went, if the batteries went, if the sunshine went, it would run by hand crank.

Besides the radio, the appliances—stove, tiny fridge, water heater—all ran on propane. The wood-stove was similar to the one that Otis had, and could heat the tiny space for a whole day on a single piece of wood. He had one lamp, a stack of his own dog-eared library books and a padded bed for Samson when the dog chose to sleep in the shack rather than the cabin.

Ten, fifteen years ago, if anyone had suggested there'd come a time when Jed Dalloway would be content with such a simple, meager existence, they'd have been laughed out of Chicago. And Jed would have been laughing hardest.

Even though the wind was sharp, he left the door open to clear the air inside the shack while he stuck his metal coffeepot on a lit burner. The coffee inside was just starting to gurgle when he smelled the rain beginning to fall.

He moved to stand in the doorway. The shack was situated somewhat higher than the cabin, which meant that Jed's view off the mountain wasn't entirely blocked. Not that he could see anything anyway with the clouds lying over every surface like a wet blanket.

He inhaled deeply. Unlike Otis, his lungs worked fine.

The thought was depressing and he turned back to the stove. The days of coffeehouses and designer grinds were long over. Now his coffee came from a can he opened with a can opener and he'd reheat the boiled stuff until it was gone and then he'd start again.

He turned off the flame and filled a thick white mug with the near-black brew. He'd even mastered the knack of pouring without ending up with a layer of grounds in the bottom of his mug.

He was heading toward the threadbare recliner next to the lamp when he heard Samson bark.

Sighing, he swallowed a swig of burning, bitter coffee before setting the mug aside and heading out into the rain to investigate.

The dog barked if a cow got too far afield or if a hungry predator got too far infield. Other than those reasons, the dog kept to threatening growls and a general tendency of ignoring everyone's plans but his own.

A more perfect match for Otis didn't exist.

The rain was more spit than shower as Jed followed the barking, but still, by the time he found the dog, he was pretty wet.

No less wet than the redhead, who was standing with her back to one of the fallen boulders where the dog had her pinned.

"Samson," Jed called sharply, and the dog fell back, landing on his haunches. He walked past him toward April. "You're either crazy or desperate," he said flatly. "Why on earth did you drive up that road with a storm coming?"

Her chin came up. "I live in Colorado," she said crisply. "We have storms there, too."

"Yeah, well, this is the side of a freakin' mountain and it's pretty damn easy to go off the edge." His words were drowned out by the sharp crack of thunder. He gestured sharply. "Come on." There was no way she could drive back down the treacherous road now.

She started forward, carrying her briefcase under

one arm and some sort of padded carrier in the other, giving the dog a wide berth.

He sighed impatiently and relieved her of both. "Samson won't hurt you. Watch your step. Rocks are constantly rolling and they're slick to boot. Don't want to turn an ankle." Or worse.

He led the way to the cabin. He had no desire to have her in his shack. She was already memorable enough.

They went in through the back into the kitchen. "Sit down," he told her, dumping her stuff on the small table. "I'll get you some towels."

She swiped her hand over her hair, slicking it back from her face. Her eyes, blue to start with, were deep and clear like sapphire. "Thank you."

Otis was still sleeping. Jed didn't disturb him when he retrieved the towels from the dryer wedged into the bathroom and went back into the kitchen. April'd pulled off her coat to reveal a white shirt that was soaked through.

"Looks like you wasted your money on that coat." He dumped the towels on the counter, keeping the smallest one for himself. They were old. Thin. But they'd do the job. He dashed it over his head and face.

"To be fair, its main selling point besides inexpensiveness was warmth." She plucked at her blouse, which at least meant he couldn't so clearly see the lacy outline of her bra beneath, and leaned to one side to rub her hair between the folds of a towel. "Not water resistance." She sounded breathless. "This is just not how I pictured this afternoon going."

"You didn't picture the rainstorm?"

She straightened and draped the towel around her shoulders like a cape. Her hair was messy. Tousled. And her sapphire eyes were snapping. "What a sense of humor you have." Her slender fingers flicked over the water-spotted leather briefcase. "I suppose Mr. Lambert still isn't available, either."

Jed held his finger to his lips. "Listen."

Her eyebrows pulled together, creating a line in her otherwise perfectly smooth face. He wasn't entirely sure the red hair didn't come out of a bottle, because she didn't have a single freckle on her strikingly beautiful face. "Listen to what?"

"Shh."

She pressed her lips together. A faint dimple appeared in her slightly pointed chin.

Then she obviously heard it.

Otis's snoring.

Her frown cleared. Her lips relaxed.

"I'm not waking him up," he said in a low voice.

She looked insulted. "Did I ask you to?" She lifted the corners of the towel around her shoulders again and rubbed at her hair. "The opinion you have of me must be really spectacular," she murmured.

It was just as well she couldn't know what his thoughts were where she was concerned. His emotions had died along with Tanya and the babies, but that didn't mean everything else about him had died.

"Here." She stopped messing with her hair to mess with the padded carrier. "Courtesy of my grandmother." She slid out a foil-covered rectangular glass pan. "Strawberry-rhubarb cobbler. She seems to think a couple of men on their own would be in need."

That was an appetite he *could* appease.

"Thanks." He controlled the urge to get out a fork right then and there. "Otis will enjoy it."

"And you?"

He smiled slightly. "Maybe."

She rolled her eyes a little and moved the pan from the table to sit it on top of the cold stove. "It's still a little warm." She whipped off the foil and gave him a look. "In case that's of interest."

"Subtle." He opened a drawer and got a fork. Remembering that he wasn't entirely a caveman, he got out small plates, as well. "You?"

"Oh God no. I hate rhubarb."

"Sacrilege."

She smiled and quietly slid out one of the table chairs to sit.

He scooped up a healthy portion of the dessert. She was right. It was still warm.

He pounded down half of it standing right there beside the stove before he could speak. "My compliments to your grandmother." He set the plate and fork on the table and sat down across from her.

She was plucking at her wet blouse again.

He ground his molars together for a second, and then exhaled. He got up and went back to the bathroom. He pulled open the dryer and shuffled his hand inside until he found a suitable shirt and a pair of sweatpants.

He took them back to her. "Here." He dropped them in her lap. "Bathroom's through there." He jabbed his thumb. "Try not to wake up Otis while you're at it."

Her lips parted. He could read the thoughts forming on her face.

"You're not leaving anytime soon," he said. "It's not safe. Not until the clouds lift at least. Considering the sound of the rain—" He didn't bother finishing because the rain was an audible drumroll on the roof.

She still debated it. Silently. But then she stood, the clothes bundled at her waist. "Through there?" She nodded toward the doorway.

There was no danger of her getting lost. "Yup."

She sucked in her pale pink lower lip, then left the kitchen. She was walking gingerly, obviously being careful to be quiet.

He let out a long breath, rubbing his hand down his face when she was gone.

* * *

The faded black T-shirt hung halfway down her thighs and she had to roll up the long sleeves. The ugly green sweatpants were too long too, even after she folded over the waistband twice. But they were clean and warm. And far preferable to her wet jeans and cotton shirt.

The washer and dryer were right there, jammed against the wall next to the sink and the door to the dryer was ajar. She peeked inside. Heart pounding as if she were sneaking around doing something she shouldn't, she pulled out the mound of clothes inside the dryer and pushed her wet things inside. A quick twist of the dial and the dryer began softly tumbling. Then, because of that guilty feeling, she started to shake out the items she'd removed, thinking that she ought to at least fold them.

The theory worked well enough through three long-sleeved shirts and two short-sleeved. Obviously Jed's. All soft and faded from who knew how many washings. When she reached a pair of gray boxer briefs, however, theories burst in a puff and she dropped the underwear like a hot potato. Feeling flushed, she left the stack of folded shirts on top of whatever remained and, boots in hand, padded quickly back to the kitchen.

She couldn't avoid seeing the emaciated, white-haired man slumped in a rocking chair near the woodstove as she went. But he was facing away from her and she was glad.

There just seemed something wrong about being there while he slept, unaware that she was even under his roof. It felt unfair. To him.

In the kitchen once more, she pulled the swinging door shut, then sat down across from Jed. His plate was empty.

"I don't feel right being here," she told him quietly. "Not like this."

He lifted a brow. "Because?"

She exhaled. "Because, because I don't know! Like I'm taking advantage of the situation or something. This isn't a fair negotiation."

"You need more than one party at the table for a negotiation."

"Exactly."

A muscle in his jaw flexed. It made the scar near his mouth shine more whitely. "Look." His brown eyes snared hers. "When he is awake, he's not going to negotiate. Trust me on this, April. I've tried to get him to sell for the last two years. Ever since it was obvious he wasn't going to get better."

She moistened her lips. "I know it's none of my business, but—"

"Cancer," he said succinctly. "Invasive and unstoppable."

"I'm sorry," she whispered.

He looked away. "Yeah."

His expression was so carefully blank, it was heartbreaking.

She closed her hand over his arm and felt heat center in her palm and zing right up her veins. The last thing she wanted to be was attracted to him, but pretending she wasn't was getting harder by the minute. "Jed. I know this isn't easy. Does he… Do you know if he has a will?"

"He doesn't talk about it." He was silent, and for a moment, she thought he wasn't going to say more. "Knowing him, I doubt it," he finally added.

She realized he was looking at her hand on him as he spoke, and she quickly pulled back, curling her fingers into her palm. She wondered if she should warn him that there might be a relative of Otis's. Someone who'd inherit the property if Otis really hadn't made other plans. Wondered, too, if Jed already knew.

Which just made her feel even more like some sort of circling vulture.

She rose restlessly and hitched up the sweatpants when they wanted to slip down her hips. She moved to look through the small window situated over the sink. The rain was still coming down in sheets, but she could see the two sheds she'd noticed the first day she'd come up the mountain. She didn't see the horse.

She turned and leaned back against the sink. It was an old-fashioned thing. Porcelain-covered cast iron, with drain boards attached on both sides. The kind that people nowadays paid thousands for to achieve that whole "farmhouse" look.

The stove was somewhat more modern, but still looked like it was out of the fifties. There were no true cabinets. Just open shelves on the wall and below the wooden counter. A threadbare stretch of beige fabric hung in front of the ones below, but it was pushed aside, as if it were a nuisance, but not a big enough one to just take it down altogether.

She looked up from the messy collection of old bowls and foodstuffs. "How old is this cabin?"

"You'd have to ask Otis."

Old enough to be of historical value? If so, that might be one way of protecting at least the cabin, regardless of who ended up with it after Otis was gone.

She heard a chest-rattling cough from the other room and winced.

Without a word, Jed got up and pushed through the door. It swung a few times, then stilled. Despite the age of everything, those hinges were oiled and silent as could be.

It was still pouring rain, but she pushed open the back door anyway and stepped just outside. A paltry effort to allow the ailing man as much privacy as she could.

She was still standing there when Jed returned and pulled open the door behind her.

"What the hell are you doing?"

She moved past him to the table and swiped the mist of rain from her face with the towel. She opened her briefcase and pulled out the preliminary proposal that Gage had drawn up before sending her to Wyoming and set the glossy covered presentation on the table.

"Feel free to read that yourself," she invited. "Nothing in there is set in stone, obviously." She spread her hands. "Maybe most of the ranch proper could be excluded." Gage had never said such a thing, but he wasn't entirely unreasonable. "This cabin, for instance. Otis and his, ah, his assignee could remain here for as long as they wanted. Keep back enough land to run the cattle and still benefit from the sale of the rest. Whatever was in Otis's mind when he reached out to my boss? He simply needs to tell us what that is, and I believe Gage would do what he can to make it work."

Jed's face was still painfully expressionless. "Anything for the deal."

She had no answer to that. "You might like thinking otherwise, but something *is* going to happen with this land. Sooner or later. There are too many natural resources here for it to be simply ignored. At least read the proposal. I'm, um, I'm going to go now."

"You can't drive on the road in these conditions."

"I won't drive," she assured. "I can wait out the

rain in my car." She gestured at the door. "The clouds are beginning to lift. It won't be long. And I really don't feel right staying here. When Mr. Lambert is up to meeting, I'll come back."

"You are crazy. It's cold. Wet."

She pulled on one boot then the other, hopping around slightly as she did so. "I have a tank full of gas and a good car heater. I'll survive." She picked up her wet coat and replaced the towel around her shoulders with it. She waved her hand toward the dessert. "Save some for Mr. Lambert. Happy... happy Easter."

Then, before she could let common sense override the instinct for escape, she grabbed her briefcase and hurried out into the rain once more.

She was drenched and shivering all over again by the time she made it past the wooden barriers and the boulders.

She started her car and cranked the heater and huddled in her seat wearing Jed's T-shirt and sweats. Within a matter of minutes, heat had filled the interior and the windows were clouded with steam.

She thumped her head against the headrest. "Stupid, stupid, stupid."

Even though she knew it was pointless, she pulled her cell phone out of her briefcase and tested the signal. It was entirely flat.

She opened her contacts, selected Gage and quickly typed in a text. Her thumb barely hesitated before she hit Send. The message would be delivered the moment there was enough signal.

She took a deep, cleansing breath and tossed the phone back into her briefcase.

And then she waited for the rain to end.

Chapter Five

"*No. Not only no, but hell no.*"

April turned the phone to show Archer the screen and the text message she'd received from her boss.

It was Tuesday. Three days since the rainstorm.

Gage had sent the response to her on Sunday. She'd received it right in the middle of Easter dinner at her aunt and uncle's horse farm.

He'd ignored every attempt she'd made to reach him in the time since. When April called the office, his secretary had told her that he'd gone on a short trip.

"You've known Gage a long time," she said to Archer. "You've got to convince him I'm right."

Archer gave her a tilted smile. His green eyes

were full of a sort of biting mirth. "I give the man legal advice, doll. That's it."

She huffed disgustedly. "Don't call me doll. It's disrespectful."

"I have the utmost respect for dolls," he assured, not in the least fazed. He nodded toward her phone. "Gage obviously wants you working on this. He denied your request to be taken off the deal. Clearly. You may not think you're the right man for the job, but he does." Finished with his summation, he picked up his icy glass of beer.

Even though one of Archer's offices was in nearby Braden, they were sitting at a corner booth in Ruby's Diner because he had a court appearance with a client in Weaver later.

Through the window beside them, all vestiges of the rainstorm were gone. Easter was past and it was as if spring had suddenly sprung. Nearly an entire month late, according to the calendar, but who was counting?

Temperatures had suddenly warmed enough to melt away the last bits of snow. Flowers were already poking up their cheerful, colorful heads. Grass was greening. Trees were budding.

The only flies in the ointment were her grandparents still barely speaking and April's inability to both quit the assignment she'd been given or succeed at it.

She rotated her own glass of soda between her

fingers. "I should have stuck to marketing," she said. "That's how I started working for Stanton in the first place, you know. I was doing PR for Huffington's expansion in Colorado Springs. Stanton was a partner on the project."

Archer laughed. "He hired you away from your dad?"

She nodded, almost smiling at the memory. Her dad hadn't been upset about her branching out beyond the family fold; he'd done the same himself. But he'd been somewhat put out having to explain to his wife that their daughter was moving away to Denver. "It doesn't matter how many other projects I've worked on. I'm obviously not cut out for bringing in deals like this."

"Not all deals involve situations like this," Archer reminded. "And I thought you were all about the 'never give up' tradition."

"It's easy to say," she muttered. "Not so easy to do."

"Yeah, well." He shifted and pulled a folder from the briefcase sitting on the bench beside him. "Maybe this'll help change your mind."

He flipped open the folder on the Formica tabletop and turned it so it was facing her. He tapped the report inside. "Louis Snead. Otis Lambert's only living relative. At least that we could find. He's a distant cousin. Lives in Texas. Forty-seven years old. No career to speak of. Last job was selling used cars in a buy-here, pay-here lot. Before that, he spent a couple years at a phone bank. Defaulted on a mortgage a good ten years ago. Been unemployed for several months and he's in debt up to his porn-esque mustache."

"I take it you're trying to tell me he'd jump at the possibility of inheriting the Rambling."

"I guarantee he's not interested in taking over running the ranch. Judging by his past, he'll turn everything for a quick sale. Of course, that's only if Lambert dies without a will that instructs otherwise."

"And we don't know if he has one." She gathered up a hopeful tone. "You think Snead would deal with Stanton Development?"

"I think Snead will deal with whoever gets to him first with cash money," Archer said. "Look. I'm a fan of the way Gage operates. But as successful as he is, there are deeper pockets out there. And frankly, it's not going to be long before there are more developers than just you lining up at the scent." He spread his hands. "The minerals and the water? The State itself has a vested interest in Rambling Mountain. They'll be part of the equation if there's any way they can be. Maybe Snead would care about the way the land is handled. Without actually talking to the guy, it's all speculation."

He rested his arm on the table and leaned toward her. "Considering Lambert's situation, if you're really interested in protecting his interests, the best way to do that is to make sure Stanton Development is first in line."

"He doesn't want to meet with *me*! I've tried twice." She didn't count the last time, during the rainstorm. Jed may have suggested the time for the meeting, but he'd never expected her to drive up the mountain when the storm was descending. She felt certain that would have been Otis's assumption, as well.

If the old man hadn't been sleeping, she would probably have never made it inside the cabin, rainstorm or not.

"I don't know what to do to convince him to see me," she said, which just earned her a steady look from Archer.

She let out an impatient huff. "Fine. I know. I try again."

He gave her a wink. "There you go, doll."

She huffed again and rolled her eyes.

His smile merely widened.

The next morning, April drove up the mountain for the fourth time. The black T-shirt and sweatpants were folded on the passenger seat, freshly laundered. She also had a plastic container of leftover glazed ham from the family's Easter meal three days before.

The sky was as blue as a robin's egg and as she drove up the winding road it was hard not to get distracted by the spectacular view. She was becoming so familiar with the road that she knew when to slow for the hidden curves and when she could speed up through a straightaway. She knew where to avoid the potholes and where to watch for fresh slides of rock.

What she wasn't familiar with, however, was the sight of a man sitting directly on the edge of the drop-off about half a mile below the location of the barricade.

He was old. Wizened. And leaning so far forward that it looked as though he might simply roll off, right into the sky.

Feeling like her nerves were shooting straight out the top of her head, she swerved to a stop and shut off the engine. There was enough room for one car on the road, but not two, and simply walking beside the car toward the man was enough to make her feel slightly queasy. "Mr. Lambert?" The man couldn't possibly be anyone else. "Mr. Lambert, are you all right?"

His head turned and his eyes squinted at her from a pallid, lined face. "If I planned to do a header off the edge, I'd a' done it by now. I wanna be buried on my mountain. Not at the base of it down there."

His voice was stronger than his appearance suggested. But the assurance was also followed by a racking cough that had her breaking into a jog to close the last several feet.

She reached him, extending a hand but he just waved her off, yanking a blue folded bandanna out of his jacket to hold to his mouth. Beneath the jacket, she could see his thin shoulders jerk before the coughing finally subsided.

He might not intend to jump, but that terrible cough was enough to knock anyone off their feet, much less a weak old man from his precarious perch.

She pressed her hand against her thumping heart and gingerly knelt on the road near him. "Why don't I drive you back up closer to the house?" Better yet, drive him straight to the hospital, because he looked like he belonged in a hospital bed. She knew better than to make that suggestion, though.

"Walked down on my own steam," he said crankily. "I can walk back up on it, too."

She shifted until she was sitting on her rear, legs crossed like a school kid. She really didn't like being so close to the edge and the jagged rocks below. "Not sure I could do that from here," she admitted. "I'm April Reed."

"I know who you are." He peered at her with faded blue eyes. "Owe you my apology, too."

Everything she'd ever heard about the man hadn't led her to think he was an apologizing sort. "Not at—"

He cut her off with the wave of a gnarled hand. "You make a lot of these kind of deals?"

She wasn't going to lie. "This would be my first."

"I ain't selling," he said bluntly. "Was never my intention to waste your time, though. Entertainin' as it's been seeing ol' Jed twist a little."

"Twist?" It seemed a cold way to treat the man who was caring for him. And there was no doubt that Jed cared about Otis.

"Where you're concerned," he said.

She frowned, moistening her lips. "I can't imagine what you mean."

"Then you're not as smart as you look, girl. I've known Jed five years now. That man's got an eye for you."

Her stomach fluttered and she pressed her lips together. This was getting way, way off track. She steered it back. "Coming to Weaver is never a waste of time for me."

He pocketed the bandanna. "I know you got kin here. Ain't selling to your grandpa, either."

"Well, I guess if you had been going to sell anything to Squire, you could have done so by now."

His thin lips twisted in what she supposed was a smile.

A bird flew past, its long, tapered wings flapping elegantly. They both watched it circle and dip, then rise again and fly out of sight.

It felt almost holy, sitting there looking at the magnificence spread before them. Some would want to share it. Some, like him, obviously wanted to hold it close. She could actually understand both ways of thinking.

"It is really beautiful here, Mr. Lambert. I can understand why you've never wanted it changed in all these years. If that's something you're concerned about, Stanton Development could make sure it's preserved the way you want."

He squinted even more. "When I called that company o' yours, I expected your boss to come."

"Gage." She couldn't keep the surprise out of her voice. "I'm sorry he didn't realize that. I'm sure he would have never sent me if he had. If that's why you've changed your mind about—"

"Haven't changed my mind about nothin'."

She couldn't help feeling stymied. "Mr. Lambert, why *did* you contact Stanton Development, then? If not because you know about our policies of responsible development and—"

"I knew your boss's mama, once upon a time."

Her words dried as her mind caught up.

"Althea Stanton," he murmured. "Helluva woman. Was real sorry to hear she died a while back." His attention was still trained out beyond the mountainside. "Was curious about her son."

April studied his profile while her mind ticked busily. Gage's mother had died before April had started working for him, but he still had a framed photo of her in his Denver office. She knew he had a younger brother somewhere and that was it. "He's a good man, Mr. Lambert. Doing business with him—"

Otis gestured yet again. More impatiently. "I got plans of my own for the Rambling."

"Do they involve your cousin? Mr. Snead?"

Otis snorted, setting off another coughing fit. "Girl, do you think I'm stupid?" he asked when his shoulders stopped shaking.

"Then have you shared your plans with anyone?"

He gave a cackle of a laugh. "Got me a sweet little will."

Relief swept through her. Not because she believed the presence of a will helped Stanton's cause in any way. If anything, it most likely complicated it. But a will would make things simpler for everyone Otis left behind.

For Jed.

As if her thoughts had conjured the man, she spotted him and that scary dog heading on foot down the road toward them.

She quickly pushed to her feet and brushed off the seat of her pants. "I won't take up more of your time, Mr. Lambert." She extended her hand to him. "I hope things turn out well for you." It seemed like such a paltry thing to say in light of his health. "I know my grandfather would want me to tell you that if you should need anything—"

He let out that crack of a laugh again. "Your grandpa is just gonna wanna know if he's finally getting a chance at that pass of land he's wanted for fifty years."

Since he was probably right, she couldn't make herself deny it. "People like you and Squire are the heart of this land, Mr. Lambert. I can promise you. Like respects like."

He made a sound and finally took her hand. Giving it more of a shaking squeeze than an actual shake. "Be careful on the road," he said a little gruffly.

Her eyes suddenly burned. "I will. You, too."

Then he noticed Jed and the dog approaching and she went to her car to retrieve the clothes and the container of ham.

She met Jed halfway and his fingers brushed hers as she handed everything over to him. "Thank you." Her voice sounded thick and she quickly turned away, jogging back to her car before she made a total ass out of herself.

She got behind the wheel, started the engine and crept past them, because she had to go farther up the road before there was a space wide enough for her to turn around.

When she'd done so and passed the two men again, Otis was standing, obviously leaning against Jed as they slowly headed back up the mountain road.

Jed's head turned and he watched her as she passed.

She drove back down to Weaver with Otis's words circling in her mind.

That man's got an eye for you.

* * *

"So your boss wants you to stay here." Piper read the text message on April's phone before handing it back. "Explain to me again why that's a bad thing?"

April propped her elbow on the bar and threaded her fingers through her hair. "He still thinks I'm going to be able to bring in a deal on Rambling Mountain. It's not going to happen." And she still hadn't been able to get the annoying man to return her calls.

Now it was Friday night already and she was having appetizers with Piper at Colbys.

"Okay, so let's not talk about work anymore."

"Fine. Want to talk about my grandparents still not speaking? Let me tell you. Last Sunday's Easter dinner was a *real* delight."

Piper made a face. "Want to talk about my homeroom class? Ben Scalise and Lucas Taggart glued all the school desks shut with construction adhesive this morning before the bell. Principal Pope was so mad he wanted to expel them both. They're suspended for a week, and Lord only knows what sort of punishment they'll get as a means of restitution."

"Ouch."

"And that was just the *start* of my day," Piper said. She drained her lemon-drop martini and gestured to the bartender. Jane wasn't pulling duty that night. Instead, there was a lanky young man April didn't know serving up the drinks. "How is it that

I studied theater in college and end up a teacher and you study marketing and end up a real estate developer?"

"I'm not a developer. Gage Stanton is." She toyed with her own glass, still half-full, and thought about the drink that Jed had ordered but not touched. "You and I would be better off at a yoga class tonight or something. Moods we're in? Liquor and happy hour appetizers are probably not the wisest course."

"I'm sure you're right, but that just sounds like way too much work." Piper waved at the bartender again. "Christian's new," she said from the side of her mouth. Then she spun around on her seat until her back was to the bar top. "What're you wearing to the fund-raiser tomorrow?"

"I dunno." She'd left her favorite black jeans in Otis Lambert's dryer up on the mountain. She could have worn them with a dressy blouse. She hadn't brought a lot of options for this trip. "I suppose I'll borrow something. You?"

"Oh, I bought a dress that I can't really afford."

April chuckled. "Good for you." She pushed away from the bar. "I'm hitting the ladies. Order another round if you ever get the bartender's attention. If we're going to drown our week's stresses, let's do it right. We don't even have to worry about driving home. Weaver might not have rideshare services yet, but I have a connection with the sheriff's department." She grinned. "Pretty sure we can get courtesy rides."

"Ooh, I love connections." Piper crossed her ankles and swung her legs back and forth.

April worked her way through the Friday night crowd to the restrooms. She had to wait in line to take her turn and when she headed back to her place at the bar, she stopped short at the familiar figure occupying her stool next to Piper.

Her stomach sank, making her regret the number of spicy wings she'd consumed.

She rejoined Piper, who was giving her an arch look, and managed to find a friendly expression from somewhere. "Kenneth," she greeted. "What an…interesting coincidence."

He hopped off the stool, looking as tall and urbane as he always did in a perfectly fitted sport coat over his studiously casual striped shirt and narrow trousers. He clasped her hands in his. "Sweetheart." Before she could evade it, he was pressing a kiss on her lips.

His kiss wasn't unpleasant. Nothing about Kenneth had ever been unpleasant, except his unexpected seriousness. But neither did a simple brush of his hand send heat whipping through her veins.

She wasn't inclined to make a scene, but she was glad when he finally lifted his head, saving her the trouble of digging her heel into his foot.

She pulled back as far as his hands allowed her. "What are you doing here, Kenneth?"

"You had to know I'd come after you, sweetheart."

She shook her head. "No. We broke up weeks ago."

He slid his hand along her cheek. "Absence makes the heart fonder and all that. Doesn't every girl want a man to chase after her?"

Piper was watching the exchange with interest. April gave her a sideways look and her friend just lifted her shoulders.

Big help *she* was.

April looked up at Kenneth's face. Classically handsome. Impossibly neat, well-trimmed beard. The man even smelled good. On paper, that should have made him a perfect match. "How did you even know I was here?"

"Your office, of course." He rubbed his hands up and down her arms.

Interesting that her office couldn't share Gage's whereabouts with her, yet they felt free to share hers with a former boyfriend.

"And *here* tonight?"

"Your grandma." He smiled easily, either far more obtuse than she'd ever known or he was being deliberately oblivious. "Why don't we go somewhere quieter?"

"To do what? Kenneth, I thought I was clear. I'm sorry you've come, but—" A glimpse in the mirror on the wall above the bar caught her attention and she broke off.

She turned to see the source of that reflection and her eyes collided with Jed's where he stood just a few feet away. In contrast to Kenneth's fashion sense, Jed wore ancient blue jeans and worn-down cowboy boots. His T-shirt was faded from washings rather than design. She knew, because she was pretty sure she'd folded the one he wore when she'd pulled it from Otis Lambert's dryer. His hair was short and tousled and the only scent he carried was soap and mountain air.

She knew that, too, because she hadn't been able to get it out of her head.

"But there's, well, you see, there's—"

"Someone else?" Kenneth's voice was incredulous.

She pulled away from him, latching onto the excuse and nodding quickly. "Yes."

Without stopping to consider the wisdom of her actions, she went to Jed and slipped her arm through his, stretching up to brush her lips against his hard cheek. Even prepared for it, the sensation that rippled through her was more quake than ripple. "You're late," she said loud enough for Kenneth.

Thankfully, Jed didn't jerk back from her, which he could well have done. But the slow hand that traveled up the small of her back was wholly unexpected. The rough knit of her turtleneck provided no protection at all from the sensation. And the way he lifted his eyebrow slightly, it was as if he knew it.

"Sorry," he murmured, and then his mouth grazed over hers.

Half a kiss.

Less than that.

It still felt like the earth shifted under her feet.

Maybe he knew that, too, because his arm came around her shoulders, holding her close. Close enough to feel the heat that radiated from him. The man was like a furnace and for a woman who was often chilly, it was a cherry on the sundae.

"Going to introduce me to your friends?" His voice was deep. Tone intimate.

She moistened her lips, tearing her gaze from his with difficulty before looking toward Piper.

Her friend's eyes were wide.

Her heart felt like it was ready to explode out of her chest. "Jed, this is Piper Madison. Friends forever. Past, present, future. And this is, ah—"

"The old boyfriend," Jed finished. "Kenneth, I assume." He stuck out his big, calloused, square hand. "No hard feelings, man."

Kenneth looked considerably more bewildered than Piper. Obviously reluctant, he finally shook Jed's hand. "You know about me. But I don't know about you."

Jed's lips lifted in a semblance of a smile that made the hairs on the back of April's neck stand up like they'd done the first time she'd seen Samson on her first trip up the mountain. "Kind of how it goes, Ken," he said casually.

He looked past them and garnered the elusive attention of the busy bartender with a single lift of his finger. "Another round for the ladies," he said. "What about you, Ken? You look like a scotch and soda kind of guy."

Kenneth pushed his hand in his pocket. He could have been posing for a catalog. "I'll have a merlot."

Jed's half smile stayed put, but April sensed he was laughing on the inside. As if he knew that Ken never drank anything harder than beer or wine.

"You heard the man, Christian."

"And for you?"

"I'm designated driver tonight. Coffee'll do."

"You bet. Soda and coffee are free for DDs," Christian said.

"Even better." Jed's fingers were cupped around April's shoulder and the way he slowly rubbed his thumb back and forth over the point of it was entirely distracting. "So, Ken. What brings you to this neck of the woods?"

Kenneth looked from April's face to that hand on her shoulder, then back to Jed's. "Guess I took a wrong turn somewhere along the way."

Her conscience nipped. "Kenneth—"

"Happens to the best of us," Jed assured, as if they were just two guys discussing a missed golf putt.

In record speed, Christian had set up their drinks and Jed had pushed the glass of wine into Kenneth's neatly manicured fingers. With his own wrapped around the thick white coffee mug, he lifted it in a toast. "To safer travels."

Kenneth's lips were thin. He was too polite to ignore the toast, though. "Safer travels," he said evenly.

Piper suddenly hopped off her barstool and grabbed Kenneth's arm. "Come on, handsome. You look in need of a good ol' two-step."

Once again, politeness ruled. With one last look toward April, he set aside his glass and followed her friend out onto the small, yet crowded dance floor.

In their absence, awkwardness was quick to descend and April hurriedly stepped away from beneath Jed's encircling arm. "Uh, thanks." She rubbed her hands down her jeans and slid her fingertips into her back pockets. That was safer than taking her drink and pouring more alcohol on her swimming senses. "You were quick on the uptake."

He set his coffee mug next to the other drinks and she had the suspicion that he intended to escape while the escaping was good.

Only instead of turning away, his eyes looked into hers.

"Dance?"

Chapter Six

Dance?

April stared up at Jed, feeling the world around them shrink away, leaving only him at the center of a pinpoint.

His lips twisted a little at her failure to offer a coherent response, and his hand closed around hers.

Without waiting for her agreement, he tugged her onto the dance floor and then swung her into his arms. "Don't pretend you don't know how to do this." His deep voice was low against her ear.

She could hardly breathe being pressed up so closely to him. For one, there was the incredible heat of him. For another, the man had rock-hard muscles. Like he'd been hewed from the granite rocks of Rambling Mountain.

And lastly, the man could dance.

He didn't just stand there, arms around her, shuffling his worn cowboy boots an inch here, an inch there. He could really dance.

And simply keeping up with him kept her mind occupied enough that she actually forgot to feel awkward.

She forgot most everything. Including keeping track of where Kenneth and Piper were and the fact that she was going to owe her best friend big-time for helping to ease that particular situation.

When the music slowed, so did Jed.

Instead of the whirls and twirls, she ended up pressed against him. Despite herself, her hand found the back of his neck. Her head the curve in his shoulder. She could feel the imprint of his spread fingers against her spine. "Who taught you to dance?" She sounded breathless even to her own ears.

"My wife."

Everything inside her froze. She accidently stepped on his toe and her head hit his chin when she jerked it up to look at him. "You're *married*?"

As if she hadn't turned to an inflexible board, he kept on moving, more than capably keeping her moving, also. "Not anymore."

She waited, but that was it.

No explanation.

No nothing.

Which just left her with a pounding heart and every point of contact between her body and his feeling warm and tingly.

And that's when she realized that handling Kenneth would have been a much easier road.

And one that would probably be a whole lot safer.

She flexed her fingers against Jed's. "Do you always come to Colbys on Friday nights?"

"No."

"So it's just my lucky day, then?"

"Evidently."

A few more bars of music passed while she cast around for something to say. Anything to say that would adequately pave an escape without making her feel like even more of a fool. "H-how is Otis?"

His brown eyes darkened even more. "Ever Otis. What were the two of you talking about the other day on the mountain?"

"He didn't tell you?"

His hand tightened against her spine, and the space between them shrunk a little more. "Would I be asking if he had?"

Breathing evenly was beginning to take an effort. "Afraid he made a deal with me behind your back?" Otis had said Jed had been with him for five years. Maybe Jed wanted the ranch.

He didn't look unduly concerned, though. "Did you?"

"Otis's interest in Stanton Development wasn't because of the mountain."

"I could have told you that." He turned her smoothly, avoiding another couple.

Kenneth and Piper, she realized, feeling even more bemused when Piper gave her a sly wink.

"Then you *do* know why he called?"

"I didn't say that."

"I've noticed that's a habit of yours. Not saying much."

The corner of his lip quirked. "I said enough to get you out of trouble with the boyfriend. Who, by the way, is now heading off to a corner with your forever friend."

"Ex-boyfriend. Remember? And if Piper likes him, then more power to her. She could do a lot worse than Kenneth."

"Your castoff? You trying to say you don't have a jealous streak?"

"He's not my castoff! I can't help it if he wanted mo—" She shook herself. "There's nothing to be jealous about. Not when it comes to Kenneth at least." She didn't want to think very hard about the way she'd felt when Jed had said those two words… *My wife.*

She also didn't care for the way he could so easily shift her right off course. She touched her fingertip boldly to that raised white line near his mouth. "How did you get the scar?"

"Knife. Is the red real?"

Her breath seemed to stop up somewhere in the middle of her chest. *Knife?* "If you ever saw my mother, you wouldn't need to ask." Nikki Reed's hair was as vibrantly red now as it had been when April was a child.

She was vaguely aware another song had started. Laughing women were clustering all around them, stomping boots, clapping hands, sliding forward, sliding back.

Line dancing.

But he didn't move.

Nor did she.

"Otis told me he has a will."

If she hadn't been watching him closely, she would have missed the flicker deep within his dark gaze. She didn't know if it was relief or something else.

"He tell you what's in it? Where he's stashed it?"

She shook her head and moistened her lips. "Do you have a plan for yourself? For...after?"

"Until someone makes me stop, I'll keep doing what Otis brought me here to do. Keeping the cattle alive and healthy to get 'em to sale."

"It's always possible that Otis could leave the ranch to you."

He shook his head. "No."

"Why not?"

"We don't agree on what he should've done with the land."

"What's that mean?"

He just shook his head. "The only thing Otis wants from me after he's gone is to bury him on his mountain. That's as far as my plans go."

She couldn't bear it. She slid her arms around his neck and pressed her cheek to his. "I'm sorry," she whispered. "He's lucky to have you."

"It's the other way around." He closed his hands around her forearms and gently pulled them down. Let her go. "The music's stopped."

Chilled, she pushed her fingertips in her back pockets and looked down, letting her hair fall forward over her cheeks as they walked away from the dance area.

The drinks were still waiting on the bar, though when she looked for Kenneth and Piper there was no sign of them. Another couple had commandeered their barstools. Music was quickly pounding again. Garth and his friends in low places rocking through the bar.

April took one sip of her drink, but set it back down and flagged down Christian.

He had to lean toward her over the bar top to hear her.

"If my friend Piper comes back, would you tell her I left?" She pulled a bill out of her pocket and slid it to him.

He nodded and slipped the bill into the glass behind the bar with a wad of others.

She tugged her jacket free where it was still hanging on the barstool, earning an annoyed "excuse me!" look from the woman who'd taken the seat. She made sure her phone and keys were still in the pocket and started for the door.

Jed followed. "Where are you going now?"

"Home." At least to the Double-C. She pushed through the door and went outside, but stopped at the sight of snowflakes floating in the light cast off by the lampposts.

"You've been drinking."

She gave him a look. She hadn't finished even half of her first drink. She had taken one sip of the second. "Want to give me a sobriety test?" Not waiting for an answer, she pulled the front of her jacket closer together and headed down the sidewalk toward the parking spot where she'd left her car.

His footsteps followed her.

She whirled on her heel. "Oh for heaven's sake. I'm sober as a judge!"

"Good for you."

"Then what are you doing? Following me?"

"Doing the same thing as you." He held up his hand. A key dangled from it. "Home."

She swiped a snowflake from her nose and started off again. Her cheeks felt hot. Redheads' curse.

And again, his footsteps sounded behind her.

There were cars and trucks and SUVs slanted into the parking spots all the way down the block. It was reasonable that one of them was his.

"How'd you meet Loverboy?"

She flipped up her collar and quickened her step. Half a block to go. She didn't look back at him, but raised her voice so he'd hear her. "How'd your chin get sliced by a knife?"

"One of those online romances? Www-dot-getadate?"

Despite herself, her lips twitched.

She schooled her expression and shot him a look over her shoulder. "You talking about me, or the source of your knifer?"

He lifted his hand. "Hey, watch—"

Her shoulder bounced hard and she stumbled, grabbing the lamppost she'd walked into. "Oh that's just perfect." She righted her course, determined not to rub the pain in her shoulder.

"You all right?"

She rolled her shoulder, grimacing a little. "Right as rain," she assured without looking back. She realized she was starting to walk faster, but there wasn't any way to slow down without looking obvious. Sort of like pretending she hadn't just plowed into a lamppost.

Meanwhile, his footsteps behind her were steady as ever.

She shoved her hands in her pockets. Clasped her car key in her fist. Quarter block now. Parked in front of the feed store, next to a pickup truck that was more about fancy wheels and special lights than it was about utility.

"Bar fight."

She stopped walking and turned to face him.

"In Texas. Five years ago." He stopped walking, too. Right beside the lamppost she'd run into. The light shining down on his head made his hair look vaguely reddish. "Same night I met Otis."

She absorbed that. Then frowned. "Wait. He wasn't the one who—"

His lips stretched. He didn't try to close the distance between them. "No."

She let out a breath. "Oh. That's good, then. Is that where you come from? Texas?" He didn't have any sort of drawl that would have given it away. In fact, when he did string more than two words together, his speech bore no hint toward any particular region at all. "Is working cattle in your blood?"

He actually smiled outright at that. "Everything I know about working cattle came from the School of Hard Ranching according to Otis Lambert."

That smile was so arresting she actually started to take a step toward him.

"He's the one who bailed me out," he added. "Stitched me up."

She froze again. "Bailed?"

"Bar fight," he said again. As if that were the only explanation a person needed. His hand flipped. "Your turn."

She swiped another snowflake from her cheek. Fair was fair, she reasoned. "It wasn't www-dot-getadate." She rocked back on her chunky heels. "My boss does business with Kenneth's firm. He's a financial analyst."

His lips twisted. "I recognized the type. All he's missing is the bespoke suit."

She chewed her lip. His smile was so much better than the grimace. It took years off his face. "It wasn't serious," she added abruptly.

"He followed you all the way from Denver."

"Not because I wanted him to. We never even—" She huffed. What was *wrong* with her? "It wasn't serious," she said again, and turned to head for her car once more. This time, she didn't even try to measure her pace.

She hit the fob in her palm to unlock it and yanked open the door when she reached it. A quick check in her mirror and she backed out of the parking spot and gunned it down Main as if the devil was at her bumper.

Flying past the sheriff's department reminded her to lighten up on the gas at least, but she didn't manage to draw an even breath until the lights of town were in her rearview mirror.

It wasn't long before those dwindling lights were replaced by bright headlights.

She angled the mirror a little so the reflection wasn't shining in her eyes. She didn't feel particularly compelled to speed up to accommodate the driver following her. She was already going faster than the speed limit and the snow flurries were getting heavier. It wouldn't be long before she hit the turnoff for the ranch.

Those bright beams stayed on her tail, though. Annoying. She didn't have a hope of making out what sort of vehicle it was. For all she knew, it was one of the officers from the sheriff's department. And even though she had connections, she didn't want to test them too hard by getting pulled over for speeding.

She let off the gas a little, edging the shoulder in case the driver wanted to pass. It'd be easy enough to do since there was no oncoming traffic at all.

But those lights stayed with her.

Her fingers tightened on the steering wheel. "Just go around me," she muttered.

But the vehicle didn't budge.

She sped up again.

Telling herself to relax didn't accomplish anything. Reminding herself that the highway was the main road between Weaver and everywhere else didn't help, either.

The sky was black. The road ahead illuminated

only by the sweep of headlights. Her wipers were on low, swiping over her windshield and the little buildup of snow. Then waiting. Waiting. Waiting while the highway was a high hum beneath her tires before swishing again.

And still, those lights remained in her rearview mirror. Never inching closer. Never backing off.

Her fingers were like vises around the steering wheel.

Every roadside slasher movie she'd ever watched in her teens had come back to haunt her and when she finally—thank heavens!—*finally* reached the turnoff for the Double-C, she barely slowed as she spun the wheel.

Her tires skidded as they hit the graded gravel and she fishtailed through the timber-framed entrance, narrowly avoiding sideswiping one of the yard-wide side pillars.

Nerves tight, she regained the wheel as she slowed, and finally rolled to a stop. Her chest ached from the way her heart pounded and she dropped her forehead to the steering wheel. "You're a crazy person, Reed." And if any one of her family members had witnessed the way she'd turned off the highway, they'd have skinned her.

She screamed outright when the door beside her yanked open.

"Who the *hell* taught you to drive?"

She stared at Jed, speechless.

For all of two seconds.

Then she threw off her safety belt and launched herself out of the vehicle at him. "That was *you*?"

She planted her hands on his chest and shoved.

"You scared the *life* out of me!" She went to shove him again but he caught her wrists in his, holding her at bay. She twisted her wrists, but he held her fast. "What is *wrong* with you?"

"What is wrong with *you*?" His voice was just as angry. "Driving that way? Do you have any sense at all?"

She finally managed to yank free and glared at him.

There was plenty of light. The headlights on his truck bathed them both in white, and the falling snow glittered like diamonds around them.

"You were tailgating!"

"The hell I was." His hands went to his hips as he glared back. "You knew that was me. You could have gone off the road. Hit something even worse than that gate!"

"I most certainly did not know it was you!" She wrapped her fingers in the front of his shirt, wanting to shake him and shove him all at the same time. "How was I supposed to know you would follow me?"

"There's one damn road," he said through his teeth. "Your turnoff just comes a damn sight sooner than mine!"

The fight abruptly drained away, leaving her feeling spent. Her shoulders sagged and she exhaled shakily. Her head fell forward, landing on the center of his chest. "God. You really scared me."

He swore softly. "I'm sorry." His arms came up. Surrounded her. "You really scared me."

Then she felt his fingers slide over her head. Slip down through her hair. And the pounding in her chest took on a whole new element.

She looked up at him. Despite the white glare of headlights, his eyes were canyons of dark. His face was pale, his square jaw flexing.

She dropped her gaze to that small scar.

No, that was an excuse. An easy excuse, because it was so close to his mouth. So close to those lips that rarely softened into a smile.

"Don't look at me like that, April."

She raised her gaze to his. "Like what?"

His fingers tightened in her hair and her mouth ran dry. She swallowed. Moistened her lips.

She wasn't sure if she moved first. Or if it was him.

But then his mouth was on hers and she felt engulfed by an inferno. Or maybe the burning was coming from inside her.

There was no way to know.

No reason to care.

Her hands slid up the granite chest, behind his neck, where his skin felt even hotter beneath her fingertips, slipping through his thick hair that was not hot, but instead felt cool and unexpectedly silky.

His arm around her tightened, his hand pressing her closer while his kiss deepened. Consuming. Exhilarating. Her head was whirling, sounds roaring.

It was only a kiss.

But she was melting.

She was flying.

And then she realized the sounds weren't just inside her head.

Someone was laying on a horn.

She jerked back, her gaze skittering over Jed's as they both turned to peer through the curtain of white light shining over them.

"Mind getting at least one of these vehicles out of the way?" The shout was male and obviously amused.

"Oh for cryin'—" She exhaled. "That's my uncle Matthew," she told Jed, pushing him away. "And I'm sorry to say, but we are probably *never* going to live this down."

Chapter Seven

"Soooo." Piper, looking particularly pretty in a fluttery pink dress, sidled next to April. She was waiting with the people clustered in line for the bar that was set up in front of the enormous windows inside Vivian Templeton's lavish home. "How's it going?"

"I don't buy that wide-eyed act for a second," April told her dryly. She inched forward as the line moved. "What have you heard?"

Piper grinned and bumped April's arm with her shoulder. "You and Jed left Colbys last night together."

At least it wasn't the fact that Matthew had caught her and Jed kissing like a couple of teenagers.

"I could say the same thing about you and Kenneth, I think." Not a soul was paying them any attention. All of the guests passing through Vivian's front door were too busy gawking at the gold furniture and the artwork on the walls to be interested in their conversation. "The two of you disappeared before Jed and I left."

"Aha!" Piper had arrived earlier than April and Gloria and she already held a crystal champagne flute in her hand. She tilted the delicate rim toward April. "You *did* leave together."

"No. We left at the same time." They moved forward again. April could see around the people in front of her to the table where dozens of flutes exactly like Piper's were lined up. "Big difference." She angled her head. "Where do you suppose Vivian managed to get that many crystal flutes?"

Lucy stuck her blond head between them. "You haven't seen her butler's pantry. She could open a catering company with all the party stuff she owns."

"Subtle way to cut the line," April murmured wryly.

Her cousin winked. "I try." They moved forward again. "Thank goodness I see some beer bottles there," she said. "Beck'll be relieved. If it weren't for Vivian's business, I'd have never gotten him through the door here." She lifted her arm, sending a thumbs-up, and April looked over to see Lucy's husband standing near one of the windows looking as though he'd rather be anywhere else. When she dropped her arm, she settled it over April's shoulders. "So what's this I hear about you and the mountain recluse getting caught making out?"

Piper's head whipped up. *"What?"*

April grimaced. "Who'd you hear that from?"

"Oh, just…around." Lucy's eyes were full of mirth. "So? Getting busy while you're in town, are you?"

"No," April denied. "Look. We're next." She shoved her cousin ahead of her. "Better grab the beer before it's all gone."

Lucy laughed softly, but did exactly that.

Then it was her turn and April took one of the champagne flutes, holding it up for one of the white-suited caterers to fill before moving out of the way.

Piper tucked her arm through April's, keeping her from getting too far away. "You trying to keep secrets from your bestie?"

"Of course not."

"Making out with Jed?"

She spotted her grandmother across the room, laughing as she talked with a group of people. "It was just a kiss." Major understatement. "Who's that man over there by my gram? The one holding the gray cowboy hat."

"That's Tom Hook. He's an attorney. Your grandmother looks great, by the way." Piper propped her hand on her hip. "Wish I could look that good right now."

"Oh, stop. You look amazing." But April's grand-mother did look particularly attractive.

Gloria's hair wasn't as red as it once had been, but it still remained as much auburn as silver. She'd left it down for the fund-raiser and it swirled around the shoulders of her close-fitting ivory dress. Squire was in his nineties. Gloria, however, was more than twenty years younger and had a figure that was enviable at any age. Combine all that with intelli-gence and an engaging wit, and was it any wonder that she drew eyes?

Particularly Tom Hook's.

"What's his deal?"

"Who? Tom?" Piper spread her palms. "I don't know. He has a small ranch, I think. I know he's a lawyer, though. He's handled some stuff for my dad. And don't think I haven't noticed you avoid-ing the conversation."

"We're having a conversation." She tapped her glass lightly against Piper's. "I wonder what my grandfather would think if he could see her right now." She doubted he'd still be acting like such a stick in the mud. She suddenly handed her cham-pagne to Piper. "Hold that."

She pulled her cell phone out of the small se-quined purse she'd borrowed from Jaimie along with a black turtleneck and skirt, and aimed the camera toward her grandmother. She snapped off several shots before tucking it away again.

"You're going to show your grandfather the pictures? You think that's going to get them talking again?"

"I don't know. It could backfire just as easily. And it *was* one kiss." She took the flute back from Piper and lowered her voice. "One rock-the-world kiss." She shook her head, the memory still so fresh it made her warm just thinking about it. "Matthew interrupted us."

Piper winced. "Oh. Nice."

"It was a fluke."

"Getting interrupted?"

April couldn't help but laugh. "That, too." This time, she slipped her arm through Piper's. "I might be my grandmother's date, but she's obviously blowing me off. So let's go explore. And you can tell me just what you got up to with Kenneth."

"Not a thing," Piper assured her. "Only thing that boy wanted to talk about was you."

It was April's turn to wince. "I'm sorry." They walked down a wide corridor, peeking in doorways as they went.

They weren't the only lookie-loos. Attendees were everywhere they turned, and the crowd thickened when they reached a two-story atrium that opened to a fancy brick patio that led down to those spectacular grounds that had been visible from the living room.

"Holy cow." Piper was looking up at the filigreed

balustrade running around the perimeter of the second level landing where even more people were congregating. "I've heard rumors about this place, but until you see it in person…" She spun on her high heels, trying to take it all in. "He's gone back to Denver, by the way. Your brokenhearted hottie."

"I never wanted him to chase after me."

"I know. So when do you plan to see Jed again?"

April let out a laugh steeped with futility. "There's no plans for anything. And what good would it do, anyway? There's nothing for me to do here. Otis owns the land and he's not budging."

"Yeah, but he's—"

"—don't say it."

Piper looked solemn. "Not saying it doesn't mean it's not going to happen. If he's really that ill and not getting any sort of medical treatment? Even if he were as healthy as a horse, he's an old man. My dad was talking about him the other day. Said the church records show Otis is ninety-nine years old! He won't live forever."

"I'm sure Jed would rather lose Otis to old age than to cancer," April said. "Until we know what arrangements Otis has made in his will, there's no reason for me to try to persuade him to sell. I'd only be bugging a sick old man if I kept pursuing it."

"So you have to wait until he's gone?"

"I don't want to think about it. Makes me feel like a vulture."

"You think Otis might leave the ranch to Jed?"

"Jed says he won't." She chewed the inside of her check. "Gage finally got back to me this morning. He wants me to finish up a few things with Archer since we're both here in town. After that, I'll be heading back to Denver."

"I'm sorry things haven't worked out the way you'd hoped."

She spread her hands. "At least I had an opportunity to visit Weaver."

Piper's eyes suddenly danced. "And kiss the mountain man—oh. Look. There's Vivian." She gestured toward one of the staircases leading down from the second level, where a diminutive woman with stylish silver hair was descending. She wore a knee-length chiffon dress with a beaded bodice and the hand she closed over the banister winked with diamonds and gems.

April leaned toward Piper. "Remind me—we're in Weaver, right?"

"I know," Piper whispered back. "She wears Chanel suits when she goes into town. In a Rolls-Royce, mind you. And you're related to her."

"*I'm* not. It was Squire's first wife who was related to Vivian's first husband."

"Details, shmetails," Piper dismissed as they watched Vivian greeting people as she went. "Close enough. Come on." She pulled April toward the door leading outside. "If she gets any closer to us, she might ask for a donation. And thanks to this dress, I have a whopping twenty-five bucks in my savings account right now."

April covered her laughter as they went out onto the patio. The snow flurries from the night before had been too light to leave any lasting evidence. Particularly under the sunny afternoon skies. It was chilly, definitely. But not uncomfortably so thanks to her borrowed turtleneck.

There were fewer people outside, even though a bar was set up there as well as portable heaters and a long display of library books. In the middle were several large artist renderings of the proposed new library and they wandered over to look at them.

"Nick's doing himself proud," April murmured.

"Move over Frank Lloyd Wright?"

April chuckled. "That would be something all right."

While they'd perused the display, more catering staff had appeared, this time circulating with trays of hors d'oeuvres. Along with everyone else there, they ate their fill and crowded around when Vivian took center stage to discuss the library project.

Gloria, April noticed, never got too far away from Tom Hook. Even when she drew April forward to introduce her to their hostess, the lawyer was near.

April hadn't been sure quite what to expect upon meeting Vivian. Not when there had been so many stories about the wealthy widow. The woman was unfailingly gracious, though. She was clearly in her element when it came to asking for money for the project. But also, when April pulled out the check that Gage had instructed her to donate when they'd finally connected that morning, she seemed sincerely grateful.

Eventually, it was time to leave, and April drove them back to the big house. Matthew and Jaimie were still out. Squire was nowhere to be found. Gloria didn't say a word. She simply went off to change her clothes, leaving April sitting alone at the big round table in the kitchen.

When a chime sounded, it took her a minute to even recognize that it was the doorbell.

Nobody ever came to the front door of the big house. Everyone always came around to the mudroom entrance.

The chime sounded again and she hurried through the house, into the living room that was rarely used, and pulled open the heavy door.

Jed stood on the step. "Here." He handed her the plastic container from the ham and the glass dish from the cobbler. Folded on top of them were her black jeans and white blouse.

She felt hot inside as she took the items. All she could think was that it had been less than a day since his mouth had been on hers. "Thanks. You didn't have to bring them here. I'd have—"

"Otis died this morning."

Shock rocked through her.

Then she shoved the stuff on the table next to the door and put her arms around him. "I'm so sorry." Her voice was hoarse. "So sorry, Jed." She felt his hands on her back.

But it was too brief. Too little. As if he didn't want her sympathy.

He pushed her back altogether and his gaze went past her.

She looked over her shoulder to see her grandmother. "Gram…" She had to clear her throat. Her voice was thick. "This is Jed Dalloway. My grandmother, Gloria Clay."

"Otis enjoyed the cobbler, ma'am," Jed greeted. "Wanted me to tell you thank you."

"My pleasure," Gloria said with a friendly smile. Her eyes were a little searching. "Nothing like a covered dish from a pretty girl."

Jed's jaw canted. "Pretty much what Otis said."

April's eyes burned. She looked away to swipe her cheek.

"I've got things to take care of," he said abruptly, turning to go. His eyes skated over hers.

"Jed—"

But he was already heading down the wide steps of the porch, his long legs eating the distance to the dusty truck parked in the circular drive fronting the house.

"Honey." Gloria came up and rubbed her shoulder. "What is it?"

April turned into her grandmother's arms. "He's gone."

"Jed?"

Him, too. "Otis."

Like all things Otis Lambert had done in his life, he did the same in his death.

Everything his way.

He'd ordered his own cremation. Chosen his own plain, flat headstone. He'd even gotten the paperwork that allowed his ashes to be buried on his own land—a task he'd made Jed promise to handle himself.

Since the only reason Jed figured he was alive today was because of that long-ago Texas night when a complete stranger saw something worth saving in Jed's miserable soul, he figured he owed it to Otis to live up to his word.

Otis had marked his chosen spot a year ago. Despite the elements in the months since, the big red X he'd painted on the rocks was faded, but still there.

Which left Jed with nothing to do after his boss was gone, besides finish the work. He'd had to wait for the doctor to come up and certify the death and then wait some more for the mortuary to perform their part. They'd been doing their thing when Jed had driven down to the Double-C ranch.

Some things he just hadn't had the strength to witness.

By the time Jed received the wooden box of ashes, it was nearly nightfall. The ground was more rock than soil and it took more pickax than shovel to dig the hole once he'd managed to get past the boulders blocking the way. Samson lay on the ground nearby, his head on his paws. Not even chasing after a rabbit when it got curious enough to come close and see what was going on.

One box of ashes shouldn't be so hard to deal with. But it was still backbreaking work to get the hole deep enough for that box.

But at last the deed was done.

Jagged boulders moved. Earth briefly disturbed.

A plaque situated.

The words were simple. "Otis Lambert. Born here. Died here."

No dates were included. Otis never figured it was anyone's business, anyway. And who, in their right mind, would ever climb up onto the edge of earth where Otis had chosen to spend his eternity?

Only Jed, because he'd promised. Certainly nobody from town. Otis had flatly forbidden any other mourners.

In the moonlight, Jed carried the shovel and pickax back to the UTV he'd had to leave parked down the hill a hundred yards off. One last time he went back up to the ridge carrying the bedroll that was always stowed behind the seats of the UTV and the truck. You never knew when you'd get stuck out on the land for a night. It wouldn't be long before Jed would have the roll fastened to the back of his saddle, because during calving season it was sometimes just easier to bed down where the mamas were.

He flipped open the roll and sat down on it beside Otis.

He was no different than Samson.

"It's a good view, Otis."

The dog woofed softly and crawled forward to put his head on Jed's knee. He rubbed the dog's head. "I know, buddy."

There'd been hardly anyone to come to Tanya's funeral, either. Everyone had either been in jail by then or had put Jed at a distance. And Tanya's only family was already gone by then.

The day he had put his first and only love in the ground, it had been just him and a minister. A guy he'd never seen before. One who had never known Tanya. Just someone who'd answered the phone number provided by the funeral home.

In a way, this was better. Truer.

"Guess you knew that, too, you old man." Otis had never said who he'd been in Texas to bury five years ago. Jed had known better than to ask.

Samson scooted again, pushing his eighty pounds

of determination against Jed in his effort to take over some of the bedroll.

Jed was weary enough, he didn't care. He let the dog take his share while he looked up at the stars.

They looked close enough to touch.

He'd given up on heaven. But he still believed in hell.

Otis was the one who'd shown him the way out.

He'd brought Jed up to this very spot when he'd arrived that first day on the Rambling Rad.

"You think your life is so bad? You really want to end it? Stop playing around at it and do the job right." He'd gestured at the sheer drop-off. "You won't survive going over that. And there are plenty other spots down the road. Don't have to look hard. Otherwise, work starts early here. You can fix up that ol' potting shed however you want. I need someone with a strong back and tight lips. In return, you'll get room and board and a percentage of whatever profit the ranch makes for as long as you're working it." Then he'd let out that cackle of a laugh. "'Course a hunnert percent of nothing is still nothing."

"You can be glad I didn't walk off the edge," Jed muttered, resting his hand on the freshly turned earth beside him. "Nobody else'd be fool enough to bury you on the side of a mountain."

He'd sure thought about walking off the ledge, though.

But as the weeks, then the months and the years passed, he'd climbed up to this spot less and less.

The last time he'd been up here had been to help Otis paint that damn red X.

The dog had stretched out. Jed pushed with his own weight to gain enough space and stretched out, too.

He propped his hands behind his neck and stared down at the lights sparkling in the distance. Was April still down there somewhere?

Working out Stanton Development's next move?

Or had she already gone back to Denver where good ol' Kenneth would be waiting with open arms?

Jed couldn't really blame the guy.

He'd set his eyes on Tanya more than a decade before she'd even given him the time of day.

If she had never done so, she'd never have died.

And as far as Jed was concerned, that was the very definition of hell. Knowing that if it weren't for him, Tanya and the babies she'd carried would still be alive today.

Chapter Eight

The house—a generous term if there ever was one—was still sitting on the side of the mountain.

Wood still gone gray with weathering. Worn deck still lining the front side of the house.

April zipped up her leather jacket and reached inside the car for the padded carrier. She started to close the car door but the wind finished the job first, yanking it right out of her hand.

It hadn't even been two weeks since she'd made her first trip up the mountain to see Otis.

It felt like so, so much longer.

Now the only thing she could do coming up the mountain, was to pay her respects.

She made her way past the wooden barricade

and the boulders and aimed toward the front of the house.

She didn't see the rocking chair sitting on the deck at first. Not until she'd picked her way up the ragtag steps.

Jed was sitting in it. One bare foot propped on the splintering rail in front of him. He wore jeans and a striped shirt that he hadn't bothered to button and one of the shirttails flapped in the wind.

A bottle of scotch sat on the deck beside the chair.

"Do you have a drinking problem, Jed?" For a greeting, it wasn't what she'd intended.

Certainly not what she'd been rehearsing all the way up the winding mountain road.

He didn't look at her. "What do you want, April?"

She pressed her tongue against the back of her teeth, exhaling. She hurt inside. "I came to see how you are."

He spread his hands and she saw the short glass he was holding in one of them. "This is how I am."

She walked toward him. It was almost automatic now to step over the boards that looked as though they were ready to split right in two.

"My family sends their condolences."

He didn't respond. There was about an inch of alcohol in the bottom of the glass.

"When's the last time you ate?"

Again, no response. He lifted the glass, watching the whisky swirl. But he didn't drink. Just lowered the glass again, resting it against that hard, bare abdomen.

Her hair blew across her face and she pushed it back behind her ear, looking out from the deck. Weaver lay in the distance, a small town shaped a bit like a cross. Another range of mountains lined the far side, separating Weaver from its sister town of Braden. Yet up here on the mountain, they could have been the only two people in the world.

"It's very windy out here. Aren't you cold?"

"I don't get cold."

She looked at him. His eyes were bloodshot and his knuckles looked raw. "Everyone gets cold."

"Thank you for your condolences."

"Now go home? Is that going to be the end of that thought?"

"There's no reason to stay here." He gestured with the glass. "You said it. It's windy and cold."

"Then come inside." She lifted the insulated carrier. "I've brought you a meal."

"No point in trying to bribe me. I can't help you acquire the ranch."

"It's not a bribe." Because he didn't seem inclined to invite her inside, she just went to the door and let herself in.

The chair that Otis had sat in the day of the rainstorm was gone and she realized it must be the same one that Jed had taken out onto the deck. There wasn't much other furniture to speak of. The wood-stove was stone cold when she checked.

She went through the swinging door to the kitchen and set everything on the table, then went back in the living area. The wood was stacked against the wall near the woodstove. She opened the door and laid a new fire, silently blessing the fact that she'd learned how to do so when she was just a kid.

Flames were licking well from the kindling into the log when she closed the heavy door on it and went back into the kitchen. She propped the door open with a chair so it would get some of the heat from the fire. The most modern thing in the place seemed to be the phone, and it looked nearly antique. No coffeemaker. No microwave. She remembered that from the last time she'd been up there.

She searched behind the curtain hanging from the counter and found a tin of ground coffee. The metal coffeepot sitting cold on the stove was the same style that Squire always used when he'd taken his grandkids out camping and fishing.

She gave it a thorough wash, filled it with water from the tap and stuck it back on the stove, fiddling with the burner a bit before the gas flame lit.

There was a bowl of eggs in the ancient refrigerator. Freckled and colored and probably farm fresh versus the supermarket. She cracked one into a small bowl and stirred several scoops of coffee into it. When the water was boiling, she dumped in the slurry and stirred it until it foamed up. Then she poured in a bowlful of cold water settling the whole mess and turned off the flame.

When Jed finally came in, she was sitting at the table sipping at a cup.

It was too late for lunch. A little early for supper. But she'd set the table with a plate from his shelf. Folded one of the napkins from her carrier and placed it beneath the mismatched flatware that had been piled in the sink.

She didn't say anything while he studied the display. Just used two fingers to push his steaming cup of coffee across the table toward him.

His lips compressed. He dumped his glass into the sink, pouring out about an inch of whisky, she noted. Then he picked up the coffee cup. "Looks more like tea than coffee. I don't drink tea."

She smiled faintly, focusing hard on the coffee so she wouldn't get caught staring at that slice of bare chest showing between his unbuttoned shirt. "It's not tea," she assured. He surely knew it. The kitchen was redolent with the scent of coffee. "Give it a try anyway."

He took a sip. Narrowed his eyes at her. "All right," he finally said. "It'll do." He flicked his free hand, taking in the set table. "Is this part of the whole condolence package?"

She noticed again the scrapes on his knuckles.

They hadn't been there the day before when he'd come to the Double-C. "Ordinarily, I'd have just left the meal. But I didn't want you having to eat alone."

"I've been eating alone a long time."

"If you're saying that you and Otis didn't share meals, I don't believe you." She sipped her coffee, pretending a calmness that she didn't really feel. "Have you made any arrangements yet?"

"For what?"

He was being deliberately obtuse. But she wasn't going to rise to it. Not when she knew it was caused by grief. "Piper's father is a minister if you don't have someone in mind already to handle the service for you."

"It's taken care of."

She wasn't really surprised, she decided. "Otis left instructions, I suppose."

"You could say that."

"Will it be soon? I know Squire will want to—"

"He's already buried. I buried his ashes myself."

She stared, feeling a sinking sense of dismay. "When you say you did it yourself—" she glanced at his raw hands "—you're not saying you *did* it yourself. Are you?"

"I had the proper permit," he said flatly. "I told you he wanted to be buried on his mountain and I promised him I'd do it."

"Oh, Jed."

"Just leave it." He looked grim and he lifted the

coffee cup again, taking a drink. "What's different about this? It tastes—" He broke off, shaking his head.

"Smooth? No bitterness? It's egg coffee. Squire's favorite."

He shoved the cup onto the table as if he were appalled. "What the hell is egg coffee?"

"You stir an egg into the grounds. And some shell. It clarifies the coffee." She caught one of his hands in hers. Studied the knuckles that were scraped raw. When she turned his hand over, the ridge of callouses on his palm hadn't been enough to prevent a blister. "You used your bare hands?"

"I used a shovel and a pickaxe." He opened the back door and pointed to a spot beyond the two sheds. "He's up there on that ridge. Staring down at all of Weaver forevermore. Lording over things from his position on high."

She closed her eyes, swallowing dismay. When she opened them again he'd closed the door and was toying warily with the coffee cup. She knew that if he liked coffee as much as Squire, he couldn't help but like the old-timey recipe. She hadn't met a coffee drinker yet who didn't. "You could have had help, Jed."

"Somebody else dug the hole when my wife died. It wasn't any easier that way. At least this time, it wasn't strangers doing the job."

She curled her fingers in her lap. "When, uh, how long ago did she die?"

"Does it matter? Tanya's gone. Whether it happened yesterday or a decade ago."

Tanya. The name sank through her. "You married the first girl you kissed?"

"I kissed a few others between that first one with her and the last. She didn't make it easy catching her. She had—" He broke off and looked down at his mug.

"Had what?"

He didn't immediately answer. "High standards," he finally said abruptly.

April dragged her eyes away from his chest again and trained her attention on the food. "You, ah, you don't have to bring back any of these containers. If you're not up to eating now, I can package it all up and put it in the fridge for later."

In answer, he grabbed the chair she'd used to prop open the swinging door, flipped it around toward the dinky table and sat. "Why do people send food?"

She made a soft sound. "For support. Comfort. Surely that's not an unfamiliar concept for you."

His lips twisted. "You ought to be celebrating."

She sat back, stiffening. "Why?"

"He told you he had a will, but I haven't found it. Looked all day. Not in his room. Not tucked among the ranch books. It's nowhere."

"Why would he have lied to me about having a will?"

"Why bother calling Stanton Development? Otis likes…liked…yanking people's chains."

"He seemed genuine when he said his interest in Stanton was centered on my boss." She fiddled with the strap of the food carrier still sitting on the table. "I can't help but wonder if maybe Otis is Gage's father." The notion had been percolating ever since Otis admitted knowing Gage's mother.

"That'd be convenient, wouldn't it? Your boss would get the mountain without the heavy price tag. And don't pretend you didn't think about that already."

She folded her arms, wishing she hadn't said anything. "If you want me to go, just say so. You don't have to resort to insults to accomplish it."

He didn't apologize. Didn't say anything. He just drank the coffee. And when the cup was empty, he took a piece of the fried chicken she'd set out and bit into it. A minute later, he scooped potato salad onto his plate.

Satisfied that he was at least consuming something besides coffee and—presumably—scotch, she went to check the fire. The log was burning well and she adjusted the venting. She suspected the interior would warm up in short order. The cabin didn't sport a lot of square footage.

She went down the short hall to the bathroom and

opened the wooden cupboard above the washer and dryer. She was hoping to find a first aid kit. All she located amid the congestion of stuff—everything from rusty tools to a can of peanut brittle and a copious supply of kitchen matches—was a brown bottle of hydrogen peroxide that looked as old as she was. She took it down anyway and twisted open the lid to pour a small measure of the clear liquid into the cracked porcelain sink. The peroxide bubbled, which was good enough for her.

She capped it again, then poked through the rest of the cabinet, finally finding some bandage strips inside a silver metal box that looked like it had once held jewelry.

There wasn't anything remotely like a handy stack of clean washcloths. So she took the peroxide and bandages and went back to the kitchen.

He'd eaten two chicken legs. The potato salad was gone. She set the bottle and box on the counter and poured more coffee carefully into his cup. In general, the grounds tended to rest in a clumpy mess at the bottom of the pot, but she was also used to pouring through a little strainer. Which she doubted existed in this particular kitchen.

Then she sat back down across from him. "How are you doing? Really?"

He pushed aside the plate and leaned his elbow on the table, pinching the bridge of his nose. "I'm fine. This wasn't unexpected. It just—" He sighed and dropped his hand. "He sat down in his chair and took a nap. He didn't wake up. Just like that." He snapped his fingers. "Gone."

She closed her hand over his. "I wish—" She broke off, shaking her head. She moistened her lips. "I wish there were something I could do."

His fingers slowly curled around hers. "You're doing it."

Her throat tightened and her chest ached even more. It was either start crying right then and there or do something. She slid her hand from his and got up to grab the bottle of peroxide and the metal container of bandages. She pulled the rest of the cloth napkins from the carrier and then crouched in front of him. "Give me your hand."

His eyebrows pulled together. But he put his hand in hers. She cradled it with one of the napkins. "I don't think this will hurt." She dribbled peroxide over the scrapes and scratches and then dabbed them dry with another clean napkin. "When was the last time you got some sleep?"

He let out a rough sound. "You saying I look like I need it?"

She raised an eyebrow, giving him a look.

He made a face. "It's been a while," he admitted grudgingly.

She could well imagine. She rinsed the scrapes on his other hand with the peroxide, then fit the adhesive strips over the worst of them. "I wish I had some antiseptic cream," she fretted as she carefully smoothed the edges of the bandages with her fingertip. "I hope it helps. That it didn't hurt too much."

"It's killing me."

"I only meant to help." She curled her fingers lightly around his hand and looked up with dismay.

His gaze caught hers and her mouth dried.

He cupped her cheek. His hand felt warm. The bandage cool. The look in his eyes stole her breath.

And then he let out a muffled curse. "Sorry."

He stood abruptly, stepping around her and pushed out of the kitchen through the back door.

She hovered there, still kneeling on the ancient linoleum floor. Maybe she was crazy. Coming here at all.

She cleared away the bandage wrappers and covered the food and stacked the containers on the metal shelves in the old refrigerator. She checked the woodstove and closed down the air control to let the fire burn low and very slow.

Then she went out the kitchen door he'd left open.

She told herself she was going to leave. Jed clearly didn't want company. At least not hers.

But instead she looked up at the ridge where he'd buried Otis.

And her footsteps started that way.

The hill angled sharply upward, but there was a path of sorts worn into the long grass whipping around in the breeze and she followed it. Within minutes, she could look down onto the roof of the cabin. Jed was nowhere to be seen.

She looked up at the sky where white clouds skittered across the blue, blue expanse. She looked out over the valley beyond. It was so beautiful. And for all of these years, Lambert had kept it to himself.

She drew in a deep breath and started up the path again. The distance really wasn't that great. Yet it was still no small hike by the time she reached the grave situated in a narrow passage. There was no way to miss it. Sharp-edged boulders pushed aside. A small patch of freshly turned soil. A flat, rectangular piece of stone planted in the ground at one end, a sheer drop-off from the cliff at the other.

She propped her hands on her hips and looked around, her breath hard and hissing through her teeth. There was no room for a truck or digging equipment. It didn't bear thinking how Jed had performed the task on his own.

Even if he'd been wearing work gloves, it was no wonder his hands had been so beaten up.

She decided the height was no scarier here than it was on that final curve in the road, and edged her way to the marker.

Despite herself, she smiled a little over the inscription. "Well, that says it all, Otis."

Far, far below she finally saw black dots of cattle, grazing in a meadow that ran alongside the hook in a stream she hadn't even known existed. She was almost surprised. Despite the notion that Otis Lambert had been a rancher, she'd wondered whether the cattle existed or not.

The narrow path kept going upward beyond the grave and she followed it for a while. She passed low-growing shrubs. Slipped around trees with trunks more than a foot in diameter. She leaned for a few minutes against a jagged outcrop to catch her breath. Then higher still, through a patch of wildflowers growing on a sunny outcrop.

She finally stopped, standing there in the midst of such beauty. It would be foolhardy to go farther. She couldn't see the summit from here, but she knew it was still covered in snow.

Standing there on Otis Lambert's mountainside, a person could think they were the only ones in the world. And one portion of her mind recognized the pricelessness of that particular sensation.

She shook it off and crouched down, grabbing a handful of wildflowers and worked them loose, roots and all, then started back down.

When she reached Otis's grave, she knelt down and traced the letters on the marker with her finger.

Born here. Died here.

"I think I would have liked to have known you better, Otis." Using her fingers, she scooped out a hole and planted the wildflowers. "I know they're more likely to blow away than take root," she said.

"But there's always hope." She pressed the soil down. The surface was warm from the sun, but the coolness below was still evident. "Thank you for taking care of Jed when he needed it," she whispered.

Then she stood and brushed the dirt from her hands and started back down the path. She reached the small shed first, finally recognizing it was really just a shelter for the horse. There was a water trough. Feed. No sign of the horse at the moment, though. There was no fence, so it wasn't surprising. She splashed water from the trough over her hands and dried them down the sides of her jeans.

The other shed was more substantial. The door was open when she passed and she glanced in, expecting to see the usual kind of farm equipment.

She saw Jed.

Sitting on a footlocker. Head in his hands.

Her heart ached and she stepped quietly into what she realized was really a bunkhouse for one.

"Why haven't you gone?"

"I don't know," she whispered. Then she moved over to him and put her arms around his shoulders. Bent over him and pressed her lips to his head. "Tell me how I can help."

His wide shoulders moved and she felt his arms around her. His fingertips pressed hard against her spine, but then moved away. "April." He looked up at her but his eyes seemed to focus no higher than her mouth.

Heat slipped into her veins, warming her from the inside out.

Her breath was quick like it had been from her hike up and down the hillside, but she knew this time he was the cause. "Tell me," she whispered again.

His eyes darkened.

He slowly reached between them and she went still as he slowly, slowly pulled down the zipper of her jacket. When it was loose, he tugged on the leather, pulling her down until she was at his level, kneeling between his legs.

His gaze searched hers. "Are you sure?"

She knew what he was really asking. Could read the truth of it in his eyes.

She leaned forward slowly, brushing her lips softly, gently across his. "Yes," she whispered, and took his poor, worn hands littered with bandages and drew them around her waist, beneath the jacket. Beneath the stretchy knit fabric of her T-shirt.

Her heart was pounding, but so was his. She could feel it as she slid her fingers under the edges of his striped shirt. Pressed flat against the hard, hot flesh beneath.

She angled her head, running her lips along that square jaw. Down to his neck, where she could feel his pulse throbbing against the tip of her tongue.

She slowly pushed his shirt over his broad, sinewy shoulders. Discovered another small scar. Older than the one on his chin. More jagged.

Thoughts of bar fights and knives were brief, pushed aside by the sheer gentleness in the fingertips he was drawing up her spine.

And then she was shrugging out of the jacket and the shirt. Fitting herself against him was so easy, so perfect. His mouth found hers and she could no more remain closed to him than she could stop breathing.

She was vaguely aware of the constant breeze pushing into the room, curling around them. But she wasn't cold. Could never be cold. Not as long as she was in his arms.

When he drew her to her feet, she went with him. Brushed aside his clothes as he brushed aside hers.

He drew her down to the rough woven blanket covering the narrow bed, and she sighed his name and felt herself melting around him.

He rose over her, threading his fingers through her hair. Spreading it carefully out around her head. "You're too beautiful for this place." His voice was rough. Husky.

She ran her finger over his lower lip. Tears were blurring her vision, and she wasn't even really sure why. "This is what's beautiful," she whispered, and raised up to kiss him. She slid her leg along his, arching into him. Taking him in. Catching her breath at the feel. At the perfect, wondrous feel of him against her.

His breath came harder. His forehead pressing against hers. His thumb rubbing the moisture on her cheek. "I don't want to hurt you."

"You aren't." She twined her arms around him, taking more. "You won't, Jed. I promise you." She found his mouth, only to tear away, gasping with promise as he pressed into her even more deeply. Until there was nothing between them but heartbeats and sighs. Until her blood sang and her name was a rough groan against her ear as he drove them both right off the edge of heaven.

And after, when she lay exhausted in his arms, he brushed the moisture from her cheek yet again. "Stay," he murmured.

Just that simply, she felt her heart being stolen.

She nodded, pressing her head against that curve in his shoulder that seemed designed for her alone. He caught her fingers in his and kissed them.

And then he closed his eyes and exhaled so deeply, it felt like it came from the very center of his soul.

She watched him sleep until the light outside the open door of his little bunkhouse-for-one shifted and darkened.

She wasn't cold. The heat radiating off his body could have heated the world.

When it was fully dark, she finally slid off the

bed, careful not to disturb him. She went to the door and looked out. The sky was ink. The stars brilliant around a white moon.

Her bare skin prickled with chill.

She quietly closed the door and in the moonlight shining through the single window, she went back to the bed.

He didn't wake. Not really. But his arm came around her waist as he murmured something and pulled her close again.

She exhaled carefully, that low, soft murmur ringing through her mind like the sweetest lullaby.

"Forever."

Chapter Nine

When she woke, sunlight was filling the bunk-house.

And despite the blanket tucked tightly around her and the big, shaggy dog curled against her feet as if they'd been lifelong friends, it was *cold*.

She pushed up on her elbow.

You could take in the entirety of the room in one glance. Jed was not there.

She exchanged looks with the dog. "Where is he, Samson?"

The dog licked her hand, then leisurely hopped down from the bed and went to the closed door.

Bemused, she slid off the thin mattress and opened the door for him. There wasn't a lock on the thing. She half suspected the dog could have opened it all on his own if he'd wanted.

She closed the door and went into the bathroom. Equally as empty as the rest of the place.

She used the facilities and washed her hands and face while she looked in the mirror over the sink.

There was no logic to falling for Jed Dalloway.

But she knew she'd gone and done exactly that.

So fully and completely that she marveled why it didn't show in her reflection.

She tugged on the mirror to look behind it and saw the usual stuff on the narrow shelves. Deodorant. Toothpaste. She squeezed some of that onto her finger and did what she could with her teeth. She didn't find a hairbrush, so she had to make do with her fingers there, as well. Goose pimples were breaking out all over by the time she pushed the tube of toothpaste back onto the little shelf.

When she did so, she knocked something off, and she narrowly caught the ring before it could slide down the sink drain.

She held up the wide ring.

Gold metal in a distinctive, chunky weave.

It was large enough to slip all the way down her thumb. She slid it off her thumb and spotted the engraving inside the band. The letters were worn soft, but they were still distinct.

Forever.

She swallowed. A wedding ring, she realized. Sized for a man.

Forever.

It was a simple word.

And it had every singing cell inside her body going silent.

She'd been falling head over heels for him. But he hadn't said that word to April when he'd pulled her next to him in that narrow bed of his.

He'd simply been thinking about his wife.

She pushed the ring back onto the shelf and slammed the mirror door shut.

She felt an immediate and imperative urge to escape.

Fortunately, since the man was nowhere to be seen, she didn't have any problems doing just that.

She pulled on her clothes and jacket and hopped around on one foot as she yanked on her boots.

Five minutes later, she was running down the road to her car.

She couldn't wait to get off the mountain.

And she never wanted to return to it.

"What?"

Three weeks later, April stood in Gage Stanton's high-rise office and stared at him. Alarm was congealing into a hard knot inside her. "I don't want to go back to Weaver. I should never have gone in the first place. Cutting deals is your forte. Not mine."

Gage merely leaned back in his chair and spun it to look out the tall windows at the downtown buildings of Denver. "And there's still one to negotiate."

She flapped her arms. "I don't know with whom! Otis told me he had a will, but none has been filed. If the thing ever really existed, no one is claiming to have seen it. No one who's witnessed it has stepped forward. Lambert didn't associate with anyone in town unless he had to. Archer still checked with every local attorney in case they helped Lambert draw one up and he turned up zip."

Gage spun again to face her. "Snead is in Weaver, asserting he's the rightful heir. The administrator assigned by the court has already determined there are no encumbrances against the property. Even intestate, it's going to be straightforward. The estate should be settled with relative ease within the next few weeks and I want Snead on the hook by then."

April pressed her lips together. She looked at the framed photos placed on his credenza.

His mother, Althea Stanton.

His brother, Noah Locke.

"Otis's interest wasn't in a real estate deal," she said. "It was in *you*. I told you that."

"So?"

She exhaled and twisted her fingers together. "Gage, Otis knew your mother. When he knew he was dying, he reached out to her son. To you. Don't you wonder why?"

"No."

"Maybe he and your mother—" She didn't know how to be delicate about it. "Maybe they had a relationship at some point. You know. Maybe—"

He gave a bark of laughter that was entirely without mirth. "You suggesting Otis Lambert was my father?"

She spread her hands. "Well, couldn't it be possible?"

His lips thinned. "No."

"Are you *sure*? A son would have the first rights of inheritance over a distant cousin! Everyone knows your mother raised you on her own. Isn't it possible that—"

"No." He sighed and shoved his hand through his black hair. "Just because I don't talk about it doesn't mean I don't know exactly who my father was. And it most definitely was *not* a man named Otis Lambert."

The wind whooshed right out of her sails and she flopped down into one of the upholstered chairs fronting his wide desk. "Anyone can make a deal with Snead. You certainly don't need me there to do it. And frankly—" she stared down at her hands, "—I'm not sure I have the stomach for it."

"Why?"

It took no effort whatsoever to summon an image of Jed. There hadn't been a single day since she'd left Weaver that he hadn't been in her thoughts. And Lord knew the man wasn't chasing after her.

Why would he?

April had been nothing more for him than a night of comfort.

She couldn't even blame him for it.

She was the one who'd made more out of their lovemaking than it was.

She was worse than Kenneth; spinning romance out of thin air.

"April," Gage prompted. "What's the problem?"

"It's just, um—" She spread her hands. "I don't want—"

He waited, one eyebrow lifted.

When she still didn't manage to produce any credible argument, he opened a drawer on his desk and pulled out an envelope. "You can deliver this, too." He slid it across to her. "It's a donation—a real donation—to that library thing."

She peeked inside the envelope to see the amount listed on the check, and this time it was her turn to raise her eyebrows. The donation that she'd already made on Stanton's behalf at Vivian's fund-raiser had been just a few hundred dollars.

This donation was in an entirely different class.

She looked up at Gage. "That's a lot of interest in a library thing. In a small town. In another state." It wasn't the typical kind of infrastructure that concerned them. Not unless it was a housing development, and that wasn't Gage's goal at all.

He shrugged. "I've met Vivian," he said as if that explained it all.

And who was April to say that it didn't?

It was Gage's money, after all. It was his choice how he wanted to spend it.

She flicked the envelope in her fingers. "Fine. I'll deliver the check and meet with Snead." She thought about the preliminary proposal they'd prepared for Otis. The one she'd left with Jed a month ago. "Am I putting a proposal to him, then? From everything Archer said about Snead, I think the only thing he'll care about is a dollar figure."

"Straightforward money deal. You know what our range is. Start at the bottom and see how it floats. If he won't agree even at the top, then let me know. I'll decide then if we'll go higher or walk away."

She couldn't help herself. "You'd actually go higher?"

"To own a mountain of undeveloped, pristine wilderness? I might."

She pressed her palms together. "What, uh, what about the ranch house? The cattle and everything?" *What about Jed?*

"The ranch is barely profitable. It's nothing compared with the rest of the mountain."

"It's important, too." The words popped out,

earning a curious look from him. Feeling hot inside, she shrugged. "You could…could have a guest ranch maybe."

"Instead of a resort." He sounded incredulous.

"Or in addition to. The mountain's big enough for both. There are lots of people interested in having that experience. Not just, you know, your usual outdoor—" She broke off when his phone buzzed and he shooed her out with his hand as he reached for it.

End of conversation.

April left his office and returned to her own, which was really just a cubicle in a room full of a dozen identical others. She packed up her laptop and slid it into her briefcase and headed out.

She stopped by her apartment to change out of her work clothes into sandals and a flowered pullover shift. Feeling disgruntled, she threw more clothes into an overnighter and pitched it all into her car. A full tank of gas later, and she was on the road once again back to Wyoming and Weaver.

The drive took nearly eight hours, thanks to road construction on the two-lane highway between Braden and Weaver. With winter finally in the rearview mirror, road repairs and improvements were in full gear.

When Rambling Mountain came into view in the distance, looking purple in the lengthening sunlight, she wanted to turn around and drive another eight hours just to get away.

Of course, she didn't.

She just kept driving toward the mountain, pulling closer and closer until she reached the turnoff for the ranch road.

She hadn't bothered calling ahead to the Double-C. She'd left just as abruptly three weeks ago as she'd be arriving now.

When she drove through the timbered entrance, all she could think about was that kiss the night Jed had followed her from Colbys, and it left such an acute ache inside her that she felt shaky. The feeling hadn't abated even when she finally reached the circle drive at the big house.

She drove around to the side of the house where the usual scattering of ranch vehicles were parked. She parked next to an SUV bearing the Double-C brand on the door, grabbed her belongings from the trunk and pushed her way through the screen door into the mudroom.

She dumped her briefcase and overnighter on the floor next to the enormous washing machine. "I'm back," she announced needlessly as she headed into the kitchen, where she could see supper was in full progress.

A half-dozen surprised faces turned her way.

April saw none of them.

None of them, because Jed was sitting right

there, with her uncle Matthew on one side and her grandmother on the other.

She was glad she'd already set down her bags, because if she hadn't, she was pretty sure she would have dropped them right then and there.

Gloria was the first one to jump up. She gave April a squeeze. "Sweetheart, why didn't you call?"

"Bad cell reception," she lied, trying to keep from staring too obviously at Jed. She closed her hands over the back of the one noticeably empty chair. "Where's Squire? And please don't tell me the two of you are still fighting about Vivian Templeton."

"Council meeting," Gloria provided. "And don't worry. We're speaking again."

"Just not about library projects or anything else to do with Vivian," Matthew said wryly.

April smiled and managed a light laugh, though in truth she was more than a little relieved.

She leaned over her aunts and uncles to give them quick kisses and muttered a hello to Jed only because it would be noticeable if she didn't.

"Sit down, honey. We're all finished, but I'll get you a plate. Been so warm, we've had our first outdoor grilling of the season."

"Actually, I, um…" She looked over her shoulder toward the door. "I just needed to drop off my stuff. There's something I still have to do."

"What?"

"Just, uh, just…stuff." She knew she was flushing but there wasn't a thing she could do about it. She bumped into the doorway as she backed out of the kitchen and nearly tripped over her own suitcase before she managed to push through the screen door again.

The gravel crunched under her sandals as she hurried around the house and to her car.

She didn't have a destination in mind. Only a desire to escape.

"April."

His voice made her flinch. She ignored it and yanked open her car door.

Unfortunately, that was as far as she could go, considering her keys were inside her briefcase.

Which was still in the mudroom.

Jed pulled open the car door and looked down at her. Not saying a word.

Just standing there. Wearing a clean white shirt rolled up to his elbows and untucked over faded blue jeans. Dark brown eyes frowning down at her.

Her nerves were too frayed. "What are you *doing* here?"

"Eating supper."

She wanted to launch out of the car and shove him. She rubbed her hands over the steering wheel, fingers clenching and unclenching. "Don't do that."

"Why?"

"Exactly!" She shot him a look. "*Why?* Why are you *here*?"

"Your uncle's offered me a job."

Her breath wheezed out of her. "But what about the Rambling Rad?"

He propped his arm on the roof of the car, which only stretched his shirt across the flat of his stomach.

She tightened her hands again around the steering wheel just to make sure they didn't go and do something incredibly stupid, like reach out to touch him.

"Otis is gone. It's not my ranch. Remember?"

Her shoulders sank. "How could I forget?" She chewed the inside of her cheek and looked up at him. The last time she'd seen him—before the part in his bunkhouse-for-one—he'd looked as dreadful as a man could after literally burying his friend.

And despite Jed's assertion that he'd only worked for Otis, there was no doubt the man had been his friend.

Now he looked at least more rested. His eyes weren't bloodshot from lack of sleep or whatever.

"How *are* you?"

He pushed his fingers into the front pocket of his jeans. "How do I look?"

Too good for words.

She redirected her gaze upward again somewhere beyond his right ear. "Like you need a haircut." She kept her voice crisp. But then ruined it

all because she really did have too short a supply
of willpower where he was concerned. Her gaze
went back to his. Searching. "You really want to
work for the C?"

"You think I shouldn't?" His fingers drummed
the roof of the car. "It's your family's ranch. What's
wrong with it?"

"Nothing! It's just—" She looked out her car
windows at the ranch trucks. The outbuildings. The
big house might be pretty modest, but nothing else
about the ranch was. "I know it's a cattle ranch,
but the Double-C is quite a corporate enterprise
now." Everyone in the family held shares. Even her.
There were employees who were the typical ranch
hand, and there were ones who sat in an office on
computers logging this and tracking that. "There
is a big difference between working on a ranch like
this and running a couple hundred head by yourself on the Rad."

"So?"

"So—" she lifted her shoulders "—I'm not saying you wouldn't be good at anything you want to
do, it's just, well you—you don't strike me as being
particularly corporate minded."

His lips twisted. "Baby, you have no idea."

"Don't call me baby." Her cheeks went hot. "I,
uh, I have a name."

His eyebrow peaked. "From now on, you'll be
forever April, then."

He couldn't possibly know what a blow that felt like. He didn't know she'd seen the inscription in his wedding ring.

She should have left well enough alone.

"What're you doing back here?"

Of course he wouldn't expect her to return because of *him*.

She exhaled and looked down at her toes, freshly painted bright blue in honor of sandal season. The color choice might have been a mistake. "Same thing as before. Gage's interest in the mountain hasn't changed. He wants it. Period." She eyed him from beneath her lashes. "H-have you met him? Louis Snead?"

He drummed the roof of the car again. "Everyone in town has probably met the guy by now."

"What do you mean?"

"He's going to inherit everything. Man's no fool. He knows what it is worth. He's been talking to everyone in town."

"Are you still looking after it? The ranch?"

"I told you I would."

"Until someone makes you stop," she remembered.

"From the way things are going, that's going to happen sooner rather than later."

"Has Snead been up to the cabin?"

"He doesn't care about the cabin. Doesn't care about anything except selling it and everything else." Jed's drumming finally stopped. "Right up your alley."

She restlessly pushed him out of her way and climbed out of the car. There was no point in pretending she was heading anywhere. "Don't make it sound like something dirty. If Stanton buys it, the integrity of the land will be respected at least. He wouldn't be mining or drilling." She leaned against the side of the car, arms folded. "You told me once that you disagreed with Otis about what he should have done with the land."

"It doesn't matter anymore, does it."

He hadn't meant it as a question, but she took it as one anyway. "If it *were* up to you."

His eyes turned flat. "But it isn't. Otis and I got what we needed from each other. He got a strong back from me and I got a reason to get up in the morning. Nothing more, nothing less."

"I think having a reason to get up in the morning is quite a lot, actually." The pinging of his chunky gold wedding ring hitting a porcelain sink was sounding inside her head. "Humor me. What do you think Otis should've done with the land?"

He sighed impatiently and took a step, almost as though he was going to walk away from her.

But he didn't.

"It's a natural paradise. It should be protected."

"Wasn't that what Otis was doing in his life? Protecting it from everyone else?"

"You didn't know Otis long enough. Hoarding was more the intent. And protecting doesn't mean it shouldn't be enjoyed." He waved an arm toward the mountain that stood sentinel in the distance. "Everyone around here looks up at that mountain and not a single one enjoys it up close. They can't experience it. They can't hike to the summit where the snow never entirely melts. They can't look down in a lake that is so clear it's unearthly."

"You sound like an environmentalist. What exactly *did* you do before Otis? Before Texas?"

A muscle in his jaw flexed. "Took a lot of money from a lot of people and turned it into a lot more."

"What?"

"I was an investment banker."

If he'd told her he'd been an acrobat in a circus, she wouldn't have been more stunned.

He touched his finger to her chin, making her jump. "Close your mouth, Miss Reed."

She clenched her teeth, swallowing hard. Her cheeks felt positively fiery. She lifted her chin, breaking the contact. "Where?"

"Chicago."

"I meant what company."

He exhaled. "Does it matter?"

She shook her head, still feeling stunned. "How'd you go from investment banking to—" she waved her hand "—to the school of ranching according to Otis?"

He propped his hands on his hips and exhaled.

His profile was sharp against the thinning sunlight. "That is a long story."

It was pathetic how easily she forgot that she needed to keep her distance. To stay objective. "I don't mind a long story."

She knew he wasn't going to say more, though. She could read it in his expression even before he lifted his hand and rubbed his thumb along her chin. "Why'd you disappear that morning?"

Her ears suddenly filled with the rushing sound of nerves. "You were the one who was gone when I woke up."

"I was in the cabin."

She hadn't looked. She hadn't hung around one second longer than it had taken to dress and escape.

It wouldn't have changed anything, though.

She might have fallen for Jed.

But to him, she'd just been a substitute for the wife he lost.

She made herself shrug. "You know how it is." She forced out the light words. "Mornings after are always so awkward." As if she'd ever had a morning after with someone. She was no virgin. But she'd never ever spent an entire night with someone. Never had cared enough to even want to. "It's not like we'll have a repeat. I was doing us both a favor."

Something in his eyes flickered. "Right. No need for things to get awkward. Handy when a girl already gets that."

She forced her smile to stay put as he walked away, heading toward a dusty pickup truck. A truck she recognized, having seen it often enough parked at the roadblock leading up to the Rambling Rad.

The second that truck started to move, wheels crunching over the gravel, her facade dissolved.

She blinked against the tears burning her eyes as she looked toward Otis's mountain.

She wished, yet again, that she'd never met her boss, the old man buried on a mountain, or Jed.

Chapter Ten

The wildflowers had spread. In just three weeks, they had nearly filled in all of the turned-over earth of Otis's grave.

By the time summer ended, Jed knew the only evidence of the grave would be the stone marker.

He poured the water he'd brought up to the ridge over the wildflowers. "Figure this is just the way you wanted it, Otis. Being one with your mountain."

When the metal bucket was empty, he flipped it over and sat down on it.

He knew that April had to have been the one who'd planted the sprig of flowers after Otis died. He'd seen them, looking spindly and frail among the rocky soil that day she'd disappeared on him. It wasn't something he'd have thought to do.

But there they'd been. Heads of purple and red barely hanging on in the constant breeze tugging at them.

He'd brought up water that day. Tamped down the roots again. Added a little more soil and moved some rocks to provide some protection from the wind.

Since there hadn't been any rain, he'd done the same thing every day. And now the wildflowers were taking over all on their own. No longer in need of protection from the wind. Riotous, colorful weeds that would go to seed and sprout up again thicker than ever, finding life among the granite, in a cycle that Jed hoped would never end.

"She came back, Otis." He squinted into the sun, looking down at the creek-side meadow where most of the cows were contained. Babies were dropping regularly, keeping him even busier than usual. Fortunately, there hadn't been any orphans this season. It was a first, though Jed was too practical to expect the luck to continue. "That company of hers still wants your land." He wasn't going to think about anything else where she was concerned. Definitely not the fact that aside from Tanya, April was the only woman he'd ever wanted in his bed come morning.

And even though he'd fallen into the habit of

talking more to Otis now that he was gone than he ever had when he was alive, there was no way Jed would share the fact that, out of all the women he'd been with since his wife died, being with April was the only time he hadn't had a single thought about his past at all.

He pinched his nose to rid himself of the thought.

"Not sure she's gonna get a deal, though," he finally continued aloud. "Snead's already bragging in town that he's got a mining company lined up. You always told me you never wanted to see mining on your mountain."

Jed had heard the cousin showed up a week after Otis died. He wasn't inclined to think much of the guy. He'd never tried to see Otis in the five years Jed had known him. But then Jed supposed he wasn't really in a position to judge another man's character when his own hadn't been anything to write home about.

"Court's sending someone up here from an auction house over in Braden," he went on. "Make an assessment of the place. Your stuff'll go to auction and there's not a damn thing I can do about it. If you've got any power on that side where you're at, it would be helpful if you produced that will you claimed you had. And if it was just a line of bull, then nudge April to the head of the line where Snead's concerned. Otherwise, God knows what's going to happen to this place." A small grave on a high ridge above a few weather-beaten shacks would be easily forgotten.

The sound of a vehicle carried up to the ridge and Jed reluctantly stood. Otis hadn't had much in the way of possessions. But Jed still didn't look forward to a stranger picking and poking through, deciding what sort of value any of it might bring.

He leaned over and tugged a flower away from the marker and tossed it aside. The breeze caught it and carried it over the side of the ridge. "See you tomorrow, old man."

His daily treks up and down the ridge had worn down the long grass even more, making the narrow path easily noticeable from the cabin. When he reached Rufus where he'd left him, ground-tied halfway up, he could see a white sedan parked down at the roadblock. He muttered a curse as he grabbed the reins and swung up in the saddle. He clucked softly and the horse agreeably plodded the rest of the way down.

He was pulling off the saddle when he heard the footsteps on the rocky road. He finished with the horse and headed over to the cabin to find the visitor already poking around inside.

Where was Samson when he needed him? Jed deliberately let the wind slam the door shut just to watch the guy jump.

The skinny man quickly set down Otis's vintage radio. "I didn't realize someone was here."

The guy had a ferret face. No chin. Thin lips mostly hidden by a mustache straight out of the '70s, and a green suit to match. "I didn't realize the auction house sent people who don't know how to knock."

"Auction house." The guy looked like he'd been born with a sneer on his face. "Nothing here worth anything. Always heard Otis was a cheap bastard."

"Let me guess." Jed's voice went flat. "You're Snead. Hate to tell you, pal, but you haven't inherited this place yet."

"Matter of time." Snead headed toward the hallway but Jed stepped in his way.

"Until then, you're trespassing."

Snead was nearly as tall as Jed, but about fifty pounds lighter. His mustache curled. "You're the help, I suppose."

"I'll take being the help over being a relative who only comes out of the woodwork when there's a little money to be had."

"*Little* money." Snead laughed. "You're as stupid as Otis was if you think that small."

Jed grabbed the man's arm and pushed him toward the door.

"Hey!" Snead tried shaking him off. "This is assault."

"Trespassing," Jed reminded. He yanked open the door.

"Oh!" April stood on the other side, her blue eyes

wide. Samson was sitting there beside her, looking like some damn lapdog, flapping his tail against the wood deck. "I was just, ah, just going to knock." She took in Snead and the handful of skinny arm that Jed held.

Some things were inevitable. Her meeting Otis's cousin was one of them. "Snead here was just leaving," Jed said.

Her quick gaze ran over Otis's presumed heir. "Mr. Snead. I just left a message for you at the motel. I'm April Reed." She whipped out a business card so fast that Jed nearly missed it. "Stanton Development."

"Save the business meeting for another time," he advised, and pushed Snead past her. "Preferably when he's not trespassing." He frog-marched the intruder down the steps, ignoring the man's cursing and pitiful attempts to wrestle free.

Samson finally seemed to remember he didn't like strangers and circled around them, teeth baring as he growled around Snead's legs.

Snead kicked out at the dog and missed. "Keep that dog away from me!"

"That's what happens when you trespass. And try to kick him again and see what I do."

"First thing I'm going to do is fire your ass," Snead threatened. "Then we'll see who's trespassing."

Jed didn't release the man until he was within spitting distance of the boulders on the road. "Don't come back until then," he suggested. "Otherwise, the next time I'll give you the Otis treatment and fill you up with birdshot."

Snead had the good sense, at least, not to press his luck. He scurried around the wood barriers, further cementing the whole ferret similarity.

Between April's red car and Otis's old pickup, Snead would have a helluva time maneuvering his car to point down the road.

Jed wasn't sure he cared if the guy went off the edge in the process or not.

He left him to it and whistled to the dog. Samson wagged his tail and shot off ahead of him, back up to the cabin.

When he got there, April was sitting on one of the deck steps the same way she'd done the first time she'd come to see Otis. Only this time her long legs weren't encased in denim and sexy boots. They were bare beneath the hem of the flowered dress she wore. Long and sleek. Toned.

She had a little scar on her right knee. Earned in a bicycle tumble when she was twelve. He knew the shape of it. Knew the taste of it.

The night before, her dress had sported red flowers.

Today's version was splashed with yellow.

And it annoyed the hell out of him that all he could think was how easy it would be to push his hands beneath that loose fabric and explore the beauty beneath.

Because one night with her hadn't been nearly enough.

She'd made it clear she wasn't thinking along those lines at all, but even if she were, what good would it do?

She was lovely and ambitious and young and could swing the world by the tail if she wanted.

What did he have to offer?

Not one damn thing.

He had less now than he'd had when he'd fallen for Tanya.

His mood darkened. "Surprised you're not chasing him down to pitch your offer." He stepped around April and the dog who'd made himself right at home at the base of her feet. "Or is that the reason you're up here in the first place? You heard he was coming here?"

She followed him inside and Jed was surprised that Samson didn't come in right on her heels since the dog seemed so enamored.

"No, I didn't know he was up here." She sounded impatient.

"Then what do you want?"

She seemed to deliberately relax. Her eyes half closed for a moment. He heard her breathing. Saw her shoulders wriggle slightly. Saw the edge of lace peek out briefly where the scooped neckline of her dress rested against her breasts.

Then she spread her palms. "I heard about the

auction company," she finally said, sounding carefully calm. "You mentioned it at dinner last night. My grandmother told me about it this morning."

"So?"

Her hands lowered. Smoothed down the sides of her dress. "So I...I thought you might want some help."

"With what? Watching a stranger decide if this—" he lifted an ashtray that could have been an antique or a dime store castoff for all he knew "—is worth being auctioned off or if it should hit the trash pile? Yeah, that's a task sure to wear out anyone."

She looked pained. "God forbid if I suggested that you might need a friend. Moral support."

He dropped the ashtray back onto the dusty table. "Nobody came for moral support when my wife died." He blamed his admission on her blue eyes. Because looking into them was like looking off the side of Rambling Mountain into clear, perfect sky.

He'd gotten over the desire to step off that side a long time ago.

Falling into that abyss of blue looking back at him felt nearly as dangerous.

He was familiar enough with the art of a one-night stand. He'd had enough of them since Tanya. But April Reed, for all her blitheness about sleeping with him, didn't strike him as the type.

"How did she die?"

His jaw felt tight. "Why?"

"You keep bringing her up. Usually a mark of someone who needs to talk about something."

"I don't need to talk about her. It's just this—" he gestured sharply "—this time of year. Otis. All of it."

Feeling hemmed in, he went out onto the porch.

April followed. "Maybe you do need to talk," she suggested quietly. "Bottling things up only makes it worse."

"You're an expert on it, are you?"

Her vibrant hair blew across her face in a sudden gust that also tugged dangerously at the hem of her lightweight dress. "Don't have to be an expert to understand a basic principle." When she finished gathering her hair in one hand, he could see her eyes had darkened. "It's not good to bottle up any kind of emotion."

"What're you bottling?"

Her gaze shifted. "Besides frustration with Otis and his will or nonwill?" She shrugged and let go of her hair to hold her dress down around her thighs instead.

He clenched his teeth and looked away, only to spot another newcomer heading up the road. This one was a woman with gray sausage curls, toting a satchel in one hand and pulling a rolling case behind her on the uneven ground.

"Perfect," he muttered, and whistled for Samson. The dog veered, chasing back behind the house.

The woman had spotted him and was waving the bag. "Mr. Dalloway?"

He heaved a sigh and lifted his hand.

"Oh goodness." She was wheezing a little as she drew nearer to the house. "Didn't think I was ever going to make it up here. I'm Eleanor with—" she paused to yank her rolling case over a bump "—with Braden Auction House. I'm sorry I'm running late for our appointment." She yanked at her case again. "Another accident on that cursed highway from Braden."

As much as he wasn't looking forward to this, he still went down to help her with her load.

"Oh, thank you." She gratefully passed over the handle for the rolling case. "That highway is nearly as bad as the road you've got coming up here." She clucked her tongue. "Felt my life passing on a few of those turns, I don't mind telling you."

He didn't bother trying to roll the case over the rocky path. He just picked it up and carried it under one arm while he took Eleanor's elbow with his other hand. "Watch the steps," he warned. "Have a few bad boards."

"Thank you, dear." She patted his hand with hers. "So nice to meet a gentleman."

He nearly choked and glanced down the mountain toward the meadow. He'd give his right arm to be down checking the mamas rather than up here dealing with the auction house. He'd already been down to the meadow once that morning just after dawn, checking the pregnant cows. It was a trip he was able to make more than once a day, now that he didn't have to stick so close to the cabin for Otis's sake.

Otis was gone. But his calf crop was better than it had ever been. Only Otis would have appreciated the irony of that.

Jed automatically guided Eleanor past the deck board that was splintered all the way through.

"Oh." Eleanor had obviously spotted April standing near the door of the cabin. "You must be Mrs. Dalloway. I'm—"

April's eyes were wide as they caught his and a blush bloomed on her cheeks. "No, I'm…I'm just a friend."

"Ah, well." Eleanor straightened her shoulders and inhaled deeply. "Friends are a welcome thing, too, at times like these." She thrust out her hand. "Eleanor with Braden Auction House."

"April Reed."

"Any relation to Morton Reed?"

April shook her head. "Um, no. Sorry."

"Well, don't be," Eleanor assured. "Pharmacist over in Braden. Died last year. Donated his estate to an ostrich farm out west somewhere even though he had an ex-wife, two grown children and seven grandchildren." She shook her head, clearly thinking the matter unfathomable as she stepped past April through the door.

Jed followed her, setting the case on the brick hearth surrounding the cold woodstove. He was achingly aware of April coming inside, too.

"Thank you, dear." Eleanor opened the bag she'd been carrying and began pulling out ragged-looking catalogs and pads. "I assume you've been in communication with the administrator assigned to Mr. Lambert's estate?"

Jed nodded, impatient to just get on with it. "Guy named Pastore. Told me to keep running things and submit all the ranch records to him until he notifies me otherwise. I sent the ledgers to him already. Otis never trusted computers. Had me recording everything by hand." Now Jed had to send weekly reports to the guy, which necessitated a trip to the post office in town since the mail carriers wouldn't come up the mountain.

"Yes. Mr. Pastore informs me you've been living here on the property, as well." She glanced up, obviously waiting for confirmation.

He nodded. "I use the bunkhouse out back." He slid a look toward April but she was busy adjusting the old radio on the mantel.

"Sure, sure." Eleanor began pulling items out of the rolling case, including a laptop computer that she set out and fired up. "What I have found to be easiest is to walk through the property with you and you can identify anything that isn't part of the estate. After that, I'll just get down to things.

"If you're comfortable leaving me to my work, then feel free to go about doing whatever you need to be doing. If you prefer staying, that's quite all right, too." Her comfortable smile took in both Jed and April. "I can do my part either way. Right now, I'm just getting an inventory prepared for the court. If we get to the point of actually going to auction, I'll make a note of items that are likely to be worth the effort."

"If you do have an auction, how does that work?"

Eleanor looked at April, who'd asked the question, but in Jed's estimation now looked as though she regretted it, considering the way her lips were pressed together and color rode her cheekbones.

"When it's possible, we tend to have auctions right on the property, but considering the difficulty getting up here and everything, whatever ends up going to auction would need to be transported down the mountain. Either to a place here in town or to the auction house in Braden." Eleanor's eyes shifted back to Jed. "But until the court weighs in, we're merely gathering information. Any other questions so far?"

Jed shook his head.

"All right then." Her look was kind. "Tasks like this are never easy. My method is to just jump right in. If you need to stop at any time—"

"I'm fine," he cut her off. "And the only stuff that wouldn't be included is in the bunkhouse out back. Maybe a couple things in the kitchen."

"Well, then. That makes it simple."

"You want to start here or—" He broke off because she was nodding those tight curls.

"That'll be fine. Are there bedrooms?"

"Just one." He gestured toward the short hallway. "Everything in this place was Otis's." There was nothing about the woman that set off alarms the way Snead had. "Give a yell if you need help with anything."

Eleanor gathered up her computer and a notepad and headed off only to return moments later with a stack of library books in her hands. "Judging by the cards inside, these are a tad bit overdue."

Jed grimaced. He hadn't thought about the books in several weeks. Not the ones he'd gotten for Otis—who'd had a liking for mysteries old or new—or the histories that were sitting in his own bunkhouse. He took the stack from her. "Thanks. I'll take care of them."

She smiled and disappeared back down the hall again.

April's gaze skittered away from his. Her hands fluttered toward the books he held. "I can drop them off at the library if you want. I'll need to go into Weaver later anyway."

"Yeah. You still need to get your pitch in to Snead."

"There's no guarantee Snead's going to get the estate."

"With no will, it's a foregone conclusion." He shoved the books onto the mantel next to the radio. "And you still have a job to do."

"I don't need the reminder," she assured him. She rubbed a hand down her bare arm. From the other room, they could hear the faint sounds of Eleanor moving about. "If you want to get out of here, I—I can stay. You know. With Eleanor."

He inhaled and shoved his fingers through his hair. Because he *did* need to check the stock again.

And April obviously recognized it, because she got a set look on her face. "Just go. At least do what you need to do."

"Babies have been dropping," he said, feeling stupid at the strange need to justify himself. "Favorite spot this year seems to be at the hook."

She raised her brows.

"It's a bend in the creek near the spot they've been grazing. Can't see it from here. Has one of the prettiest views you'll ever see."

"I noticed it from up on Otis's ridge. How do you even get down there?"

"Trail. Can't even get the utility truck down it from up here—too narrow. Rufus manages 'cause he's used to it. Once you're down, it's a pretty spot. I could take you there sometime if you want." He damned himself for the words as soon as he spoke them.

But the pleased surprise in her eyes overruled even that. "Really?"

He shrugged. "Long as you're up for a hike," he warned. "Don't know how Rufus would take to being ridden double. Otis used to have another horse, but she died of old age a while back. He wasn't riding anymore, so he didn't bother replacing her."

"I could bring up a ride from the C," she suggested. "Plenty of horses there. Guess you know that."

He shrugged yet again. "Whatever."

He looked past her to see Eleanor move from the bedroom into the bathroom. "I don't think it's going to take her too long." They could hear the squeak of the cupboard door over the washer and dryer being opened. "Here." He grabbed the books again from the mantel and held them out. "If you're serious."

"Is this your subtle way of sending me on my way?"

"Is it working?"

Her lips twitched and she took the books from him.

"There's going to be a fine for them being late. I'll get you—"

"Don't worry about it. Too bad Otis won't be here

to see the new library when it finally gets under-way."

"Didn't know one was in the works."

"Mmm." She looked at the spines. "Are you sure this is all of them?"

"I have a couple more out back."

She gestured. "Let's get them, then." She followed him through the kitchen and out the back door. But she stopped there, waiting for him to retrieve his books from the bunkhouse, as if she didn't want to go in herself.

Just as well.

He flipped the woven blanket across the disheveled mattress anyway, then grabbed the books and carried them back to her, adding them to the pile in her arms. "Thanks."

"Glad to help." Her gaze skated across his face. "You're sure you're okay? You know, with all that?" She jerked her red head in the direction of the house behind her.

He actually felt a smile. "Baby, I have survived a lot worse than this. But I appreciate the effort."

She smiled, too, though he thought it looked a little shaky around the edges. "Okay, then." She started down the hill toward the road but looked back at him. Her hair streamed out from behind her and the yellow dress fluttered around her knees. "Be in touch soon."

He wondered if he was going to have that image

of her in his head for the rest of his days. It could keep company with the last words Tanya had ever said to him.

What is the point of you?

He ruthlessly closed off the memory. "If it's to report how things go with Snead, I'll pass."

She squinted a little in the sunlight. "I meant about seeing the creek."

He nodded. Feeling that smile return. "Sure. Yeah."

She hesitated for a moment, then smiled, too, as if relieved, and turned again to head for the road.

He watched until she was out of sight.

Then he looked up toward the ridge. "I hear you laughing, old man."

He heard Eleanor call his name and he turned to go back inside.

But the smile he felt stayed in place.

Chapter Eleven

"The fines total up to $21.50," the library worker told April the next morning.

Twenty-some dollars wasn't going to break her, she knew, but still. The last time she'd paid a library fine, it had been in the neighborhood of three bucks. "How overdue *are* the books?" She unzipped her wallet, pulling out the cash.

The girl sitting behind the desk checked her computer. "Five weeks." She took the money and tucked it in her drawer, returning April's change. "You'd be surprised how many people don't bother paying their fines, though. We have to suspend their borrowing privileges. One of these days, it's going to take a credit check before someone can get a library card." She extended a colorful flyer. "We're having a sale on paperbacks for Memorial Day, if you're interested. Anything we raise goes toward the new building project."

April took the flyer and folded it in half. She still needed to deliver Gage's latest donation. "Do you know how much has been raised yet?"

"Heard they're halfway to the goal." The girl didn't look much older than a teen as she leaned forward conspiratorially. "I bet you that Templeton lady just donates the rest. That's what she did with the hospital, you know. Donated all the money to have it built."

"No, she damn well didn't," a cantankerous voice said loud enough to make April cringe. "We built that hospital through sweat and hard work while that Templeton *lady* was fifteen hundred miles away, sitting in her ivory tower sipping tea and judging everyone who didn't meet her standards."

"Squire," Gloria chastised. "Shh."

His voice didn't get louder, but it got a whole lot colder. "Don't you shush me, woman."

April quickly folded the flyer and shoved it in her purse along with her wallet and smiled apologetically at the library aide before she turned and tucked one arm through each of her grandparents'. She was pretty sure Gloria had suggested they go to the library with her to help prove to Squire how badly a new one was needed.

"Let's just get over to Ruby's," she said as she tried to hurry them toward the door. "You promised me cinnamon rolls and I don't want to get there too late. You know they're almost always all gone by ten."

But neither Gloria nor Squire seemed inclined to cooperate.

They'd needed to be in town anyway—Squire on town council business and Gloria for her volunteer shift at the hospital where she'd once been a nurse. Gloria had suggested breakfast at the diner when they'd learned April was heading to the library.

But now, Squire had planted the tip of his hickory walking stick as though he didn't plan to go another inch.

And Gloria, arms akimbo, was glaring up at him. "You're impossible." Her tone was as hot as the glint in her eyes. "You can't let a simple comment pass without exploding with self-righteousness."

"That woman—"

"Stop! Just stop." Gloria's hand slashed the air. "This fixation you have against Vivian Templeton is out of hand, Squire! It was more than sixty years ago!" She didn't seem to care that they were drawing attention any more than Squire did. "And you behave as though it was just yesterday. I am fed up. You want to work yourself into a stroke or a heart attack? Is that what you want?" She jabbed her finger into his chest. "Well?"

"I want you to stop poking me like I'm that bread dough you make," he said through his teeth. "And I don't give a flying damn how long ago it was. You want to take that woman's side over *mine*? Is that the kind of wife I have?"

"Is that the kind of *husband* I have?" She waved her arms. "I want peace, you stubborn fool. Vivian Templeton is in this town to stay and no amount of you cussing and fussing about it is going to change that."

"Fool, am I?" Squire looked so incensed that April took a concerned step toward him but she froze under the slice of icy blue he cut her way. "Maybe after all these years, you're thinking you want a taste of something different! Someone more your age!"

Gloria reared back. "What is *that* supposed to mean?"

"I know you've been meeting up with Tom Hook. You think I'm blind as well as old?"

Gloria's hand flashed out. The slap she gave Squire sounded loud in the hushed silence of the library.

April inhaled sharply, but no air seemed to come with it.

Her grandparents glared at one another for a moment that seemed to stretch into painful eternity.

Gloria was the first to look away. She shook her head. "Squire, I don't even know what to say to you now." Her voice was husky. "That you could even think—" She broke off again. She looked at April. "I'm sorry, sweetheart."

Then she gave Squire a final angry look and stormed out of the library.

Her grandfather's knuckles were white around his walking stick.

"Squire." She tentatively touched his arm. "Grandpa, you have to go after her."

His eyes were like flint. The imprint of her grandmother's hand looked red against his flexing jaw. "Do I?"

She gaped, feeling helpless.

Then she felt her knees weaken with relief when he strode out of the library, using the walking stick more to whack the door as he went through than as any real support.

She hurried out the door herself and then her knees didn't feel relieved at all.

Because Squire had *not* followed Gloria.

Her grandparents had gone in entirely separate directions.

On the street only fifty feet away, a bus was letting off a horde of chattering preschoolers, who were being ushered toward the library by a handful of adults.

She leaned against the side of the building, shoving her fingers through her hair and closing her eyes. If only she'd told her grandparents that she'd meet them at Ruby's. Or if she'd just come to the library *after* Ruby's. They'd all come in separate vehicles anyway because they were going separate ways after the diner.

Now, *separate* had taken on a whole new meaning. "April?"

Her eyes flew open and she stared at Jed, who was walking up the sidewalk. "What're you doing here?"

He lifted one hand and she realized he was carrying a book. Another library book. "Found it under Otis's bed. Are you all right? You look like you're about to be sick."

She wiped her hand over her face. She wasn't sure he wasn't right. "M-my—" She had to clear her throat. "My grandparents just had a…a horrible argument."

She bent forward from her waist, lowering her head. All she needed to cap the morning was to vomit her brains out on the grass outside the town library in front of Jed and a bunch of little kids.

His hand touched her shoulder. Slid over her back.

She was grateful that he didn't offer up the usual platitudes.

"She slapped him," she whispered. "I bet she's never slapped anyone in her life. And he, God, he just—" She closed her eyes. Remembering the photograph she'd taken of her grandmother looking like a million dollars, standing and laughing at Vivian's fund-raiser party alongside Tom Hook. Thank God she'd never shown it to Squire.

"Come on." Jed's hand reached her waist just as the first of the kids reached the library door. "Let's get you out of here at least."

She straightened and blew out a long breath. "We were going to go to Ruby's," she told him as they walked around the swirling mass of children. "For breakfast."

He lifted a brow and she immediately shook her head. "No way. Not now."

His hand slid away from her waist but only to wrap around hers. "Somewhere else, then."

She realized he was heading toward his truck, where it was parked on the street. "But your book—"

"It's more than a month overdue. What's another day?"

What *was* another day?

Feeling sick at heart, she climbed up onto the passenger seat after he'd opened the door and shoved aside a pile of clothes. "What's all that," she asked once he'd gotten behind the wheel.

He glanced at the clothes. "Some of Otis's stuff. Taking it to the donation place. Don't know if it's allowed—" he air-quoted the word "—or not and don't care. Eleanor already said none of it would go to auction and I'll be damned if I'll leave it for Snead."

Her heart squeezed. She looked at him. "I should

have asked. How did everything go after I left yesterday?"

His brows pulled together in a quick frown. "Don't worry about it. It was fine." He put the truck in gear and waited for a slow-moving tractor to lumber past before pulling out onto the street. "What'd they argue about?"

She told him. "I've never seen either one of them so angry. They have to get over it, right? I mean they've been together forever. People like them don't…don't—" She couldn't even finish the untenable thought.

His hand squeezed hers.

But then he didn't let go and return his hand to the wheel. He just kept his hand on hers. Right there, atop the console separating his seat from hers.

Her chest ached anew and she looked out the window, not really caring all that much where they went. She wanted to ask him if he'd decided about taking the job at the Double-C. Only she wasn't really sure she was ready to hear the answer. If he did take the job, it meant a possibility of running into him when she visited. If he didn't, then it meant who knew what?

Would he stay in Weaver?

Would he leave altogether?

"Heard that the court will be making a decision on the estate soon."

She startled. "This quickly?"

"He died nearly a month ago. Once Snead inherits, you'd better be ready to act fast."

She chewed the inside of her cheek. "And what about you?"

His hand finally moved back to the wheel as he turned off the main street, slowing to a stop behind a school bus that had its red lights flashing. "I sure as hell don't have the money to buy it." He shook his head. "Maybe once," he murmured as the bus started moving ahead of them. "But those days are long gone."

She gave him a sharp look. "What happened, Jed? Really? Why did you end up here in Weaver at all, when you had a career—"

"And a wife and two babies on the way?"

She inhaled sharply. Babies. She mouthed the word soundlessly.

His hands were wrapped tight around the steering wheel, reminding her too vividly of Squire's grip on his walking stick and he was silent so long she was certain he wouldn't say more.

But then he did. In a flat tone that was all the more wrenching for its lack of emotion. "I had everything. And instead of tending to it all, I worried too much about getting more. And in the end, I lost everything that mattered." His thumb started drumming the steering wheel. His focus straight ahead through the windshield. "It was a car accident. One stupid car accident like a hundred others just like it. She was on her cell phone. Texting."

"Oh, Jed."

His jaw canted. "She was four months along. Didn't know it was twins until the autopsy."

She pressed her lips together, choking down the dismay rising in her.

"Eight years ago last March," he said. "Feels like yesterday sometimes." He turned the wheel again, and she realized he'd pulled into a small strip mall near Shop-World. He found a parking spot but didn't turn off the engine. "She was texting me," he said in that flat, emotionless tone. "Wanting to know why I'd missed her appointment at the obstetrician's." He finally looked at April. "Well?"

It took her a moment to realize the glint in his eyes was challenge. "I'm sorry." Her tongue felt thick. "I'm sorry for all that loss. That pain."

"That's all you have to say?"

She spread her hands. "I don't know what—"

"Working." The word was clipped. "I was working. Trying to redeem myself from a career that was already in the gutter."

"Stop." She closed her hands over the cords standing out in his forearm and squeezed.

"Don't want to hear it was my fault that she died? Maybe you'd rather hear about the kid born and raised on the wrong side of Chicago who dared to set his eye on the daughter of the man who paid his father to keep the hedges clipped and the pool clean—"

She reached across the console and laid her palm against his jaw. "I know you loved her," she said carefully. "And I'm sorry you lost her. Lost that future. And that is *all* I am saying."

She could feel the muscle in his jaw working beneath her palm. His eyes searched hers. "You'd be the first, then."

He exhaled and turned his head and her hand fell away. He gestured at the building in front of them. "Lunch counter in there. Not as good as Ruby's but they've got decent coffee." The corner of his lips jerked in a smile that wasn't a smile, but neither was it a frown. "Maybe it's the same as that egg stuff you made."

She let out a small chuckle and allowed her head to fall weakly for a moment, just a moment, to press against his hard shoulder. God help her, she was just going to keep falling for the man. And there was no hope whatsoever in a contest between her and the ghost he still loved.

She swallowed the knot in her throat and made herself lift her head. Because he'd suffered too many losses already. Because she'd seen him smile once and she was going to make sure he did it again. If only so he wouldn't forget that even in grief, there were still things in the world to smile about.

Even if it only started and ended with a good cup of coffee.

"That sounds really nice to me," she said.

Then she quickly turned away and opened her own car door, taking time to blink hard so he wouldn't see more tears in her eyes.

On a good day, April could make it up the treacherous, winding road to the Rambling Rad from the big house in just under an hour. Driving one of the Double-C trucks with a horse trailer on the hitch, it took her twice that long, particularly when she had to make a stop at Vivian Templeton's house to deliver Gage's check. The woman herself hadn't been there, but the young woman who was her assistant had been so chatty, April could have wasted another half hour if she hadn't managed to pull herself away.

But finally she'd made it to the wooden barricade and she set the brakes and slid out of the truck. She tossed the chucks from the truck bed behind the wheels of the trailer for good measure, then opened the gate to back Daisy down the ramp.

The horse was her grandmother's favorite mount. Reliable. Unfailingly easygoing. She was surefooted and rarely spooked. Which to April felt like the perfect choice to take down a path that was too narrow to accommodate a UTV.

She tied the horse to the trailer while she pulled

out the tack. She was just tightening the cinch when Daisy nickered softly and shifted.

A moment later, Samson ran around them both, giving Daisy's hooves plenty of berth.

"Good-looking horse," Jed said.

April pulled down the stirrup from where she'd tucked it over the saddle horn and patted the horse's gleaming brown coat. "She is. This is Daisy." She finally looked over at Jed. Even prepared, the sight of him caused something in her stomach to flutter around like a caged bird. It was the middle of May and the thermometer had been climbing steadily. He only wore jeans and a white T-shirt that clung to his shoulders. "How'd you know I was here?"

"Sound travels up here. Heard the truck."

Right. She smiled. "I've come for the tour." They hadn't actually gotten around to setting a time. Or a date for that matter. After coffee—which had been particularly good, despite everything—at the little lunch counter he'd taken them to, he'd dropped her off at her car.

They hadn't spoken any more about his wife. Or her grandparents' argument. They hadn't discussed the Rad, or what would happen to it after Snead got his hands on it. They had simply sat there, shoulders brushing because of the close confines of the counter stools, in relatively companionable silence.

Drinking coffee.

She looped the reins in her hand and started toward Jed. "Hope it's not too inconvenient of a time. If it is, say so." She waved her hand toward the cabin and Otis's ridge above it. "Daisy and I will just head up to see Otis."

The sun was already well in the sky, making both his brown hair and brown eyes seem lighter. His gaze was no less piercing, though. It seemed to rove over her like a hound on a scent. "What's wrong?"

If he ever listened to the gossip in Weaver when he got into town, he'd know soon enough. "My grandmother has left the Double-C." Left Squire. The unthinkable had actually happened. "She packed up and went to stay with my aunt and uncle at their ranch." It was hard to get the words out without wanting to bawl.

"Think it'll blow over?"

It was hard to swallow with the knot in her throat. "I don't know how. He's taken himself off to his fishing cabin. She's at my aunt's. They're both refusing to talk, so—" She lifted her hands. "Your guess is as good as mine."

"I'm sorry."

"Aren't we all," she murmured. Daisy nudged her shoulder and she nearly bumped into Jed. "Sorry."

He just steadied her. "Horse likes you. Nothing to apologize for." He called the dog, but Samson was already off chasing something. "Come on." He shoved aside one of the wood barriers so that there'd be more room to walk Daisy through.

"You sure it's not a bad time?"

"It's a perfect time, actually. Any later and I'd have already headed down there. Rufus is already saddled up." He was walking ahead of her, and the leather gloves he'd shoved in his back pocket kept drawing her attention to that whole region.

She was glad he couldn't see her face. She didn't really want to be caught ogling his butt even if it was supremely ogle-worthy.

But if he had caught her, as a pastime it was much preferable to thinking about the state of her grandparents' marriage.

When they reached the top of the road, he whistled and Jed's horse trotted into view. "Need a leg up?"

"I got it." To prove it, she stretched her leg up and tucked the tip of her boot in the stirrup, then swung herself up onto Daisy's back. "Thank goodness for stretchy jeans," she said once she was mounted.

"That's one way of putting it," he said blandly, and her cheeks went hot. She blamed it on the sun and wished she hadn't forgotten her sunglasses inside the truck.

He was smiling faintly as he turned to Rufus. His dun was equally as tall as Daisy, and even though she tried to imagine Jed wearing a suit in some investment bank in Chicago, she just couldn't.

He mounted the horse with ease and she followed him past the cabin, winding around below Otis's ridge until they reached a narrow path that declined sharply through the rocky terrain. He looked back at her. "Doing okay?"

"Yeah." Even though she'd been put on horses since before she could walk, she hadn't been on many trails this rough. "What do you do when it's time for roundup?"

"Drive them down beyond the lake to a meadow near the highway. There're pens and chutes and a place where getting a trailer in isn't a dance with death."

"When you drive them, is the terrain like this?"

"In places. Needless to say, it takes a while. Even with the help we hire."

It boggled the mind. "You know, ranching doesn't *have* to be this hard."

"It does if you were Otis Lambert."

She leaned over Daisy's neck, trying to avoid the scrape of a low branch. From where they were, she could see neither the creek nor the meadow that had been visible from up on the ridge. Which meant she had no idea, either, how far they had to go.

She didn't know if Jed was taking Rufus slower than he would have, but she still appreciated the cautious pace he'd set.

April couldn't tell whether Daisy cared at all, though. The horse plodded along, not seeming bothered by the small rocks skittering out from beneath her hooves or the boulders pressing in on them from both sides.

At one point, April actually had to close her eyes and just trust the man leading them and the horse beneath her.

But at last, they were beyond the path, heading upward again into the clearing that was the grassy meadow. Despite the water rushing in the wide creek nearby, it was measurably warmer than it had been up at the cabin and she pulled the band off her wrist and twisted her hair up off her neck with it before she dismounted. Daisy immediately wanted to head for the water's edge, where Rufus was already drinking, and she let the horse have her way while she stretched the kinks out.

She shaded her eyes with her hand, watching Jed as he cupped water in his hands to sluice over his head. The water dripped off him, wetting his shoulders, his back. His chest.

She looked away and refastened her hair into a tighter knot. Then she pulled off the thin cotton shirt she was wearing over a tank top and walked to the edge of the stream. The water ran over the toes of her boots as she leaned over to douse the shirt in the water. "Oh criminy. That water's like ice!"

"Yep." He straightened and shoved his hair back from his face.

She quickly wrung the water out from the shirt, shook it out, and pulled it back on. The cooling effect was intense and immediate, making her skin ripple with chills that she knew wouldn't last for long.

She propped her hands on her hips and glanced around. The hook of the creek was still some distance away, but it was easy enough to see the cattle. Some were standing right in the water. Some were looking their way. "They're not going to be upset with a stranger in their midst, are they?" She squinted at Jed again.

"Not generally, unless you get between a cow and her new calf. They're pretty protective." He pulled two bottles of water from his saddlebags and tossed one to her. "Need to get a count of calves," he said between gulps of water. "Had three new ones just yesterday." He gestured toward the brush growing between the edge of the meadow and the thick growth of trees. "Most of them are working their way back in there. Fortunately, we've only got a dozen left to drop, but two of them are heifers. God knows why they've decided the maternity ward is up here instead of down by the lake like usual." He'd already emptied the bottle and he crumpled the plastic in his fist and shoved it back in the saddlebag.

Then he snatched the work gloves from his pocket and slapped them against his palm once before he began pulling them on. He released the coil of rope tied to his saddle and slung it over his shoulder. "Find some shade and relax. Shouldn't take me too long."

"I can help."

He gave her a disbelieving look.

She spread her arms. "Come on. Seriously? I've done my share of working cattle. Growing up, I spent a lot of summers at both my grandparents' and my aunt's ranches. I'll bet I'm more comfortable with it than you were when you first came here with Otis!"

In answer, he rummaged in his saddlebag again and came out with another pair of gloves. He flipped them toward her. "They'll be too big, but better than nothing."

She fit her hands into the gloves, wishing that doing so didn't feel as intimate as it did.

It was silly, after all. They were merely a pair of leather gloves. Had no doubt started out yellow, but were now as stained and discolored as the ones he wore. Just because they'd likely gotten to that state while being worn by him didn't mean anything.

Telling herself that was all well and fine. And completely ineffective.

She followed him toward the stand of fir trees and slipped into the shade. Combined with the wet shirt, she immediately felt cooler. She counted off cows. Counted the babies that were so damn cute it was a sharp reminder how she'd always hated leaving at the end of summer and going back to school.

She heard a sudden crashing through the undergrowth, followed by Jed's curse.

Alarmed, she followed the sounds. "Are you—" She broke off when she finally reached him crouched next to a cow that was lying on her side in the middle of a bristly bush. She was clearly laboring.

"Think she's breech," he said, trying to keep the heifer from scrambling to her feet and bolting. He got the rope around her neck. "Can you tie her off if I throw you the rope?"

She motioned for the rope and deftly tied it around a nearby tree

The second he released his weight from the cow, she scrambled to her feet, trying to run away, but the rope around her neck stopped her. Her eyes were wild as she tossed her head. April could see a hoof already protruding from the other end.

"You think the calf's still alive?"

"Gonna find out." He had the taut rope in his fist, slowly working his way toward the cow, though she looked like she was not going to have any of it. "Got straps and gloves in the bags."

"I'll get 'em." She ran back to the horses where they were still plodding around in the cool shallows of the creek. She flipped open Jed's saddlebags and found the pack of OB sleeves. She'd seen calves pulled before, with straps or chains and even mechanical calf pullers. None had ever been breech.

She finally turned up the straps and ran back to him, along with the pack of plastic sleeves.

The cow was off her feet again. He'd shortened the slack in the rope. If she got up again, she wouldn't be going far.

"Hope you didn't have to tackle her." She dropped down onto her knees beside him, forgetting about the plastic sleeves, because he already had his arm stuck up inside the cow's birth canal. The animal was wheezing.

"Wore herself out. At least she didn't choose that damn bush again for her manger." His eyes were nearly closed as he concentrated. "Not all the way turned, but she definitely needs help." He gestured. "Got the straps?"

She shook them out and fashioned the first loop. It was long. Long enough to loop twice over a hoof, pass behind Jed for leverage, and loop twice again over the other hoof.

"Thought this was a two-person job," she said breathlessly as she watched him work. The cow was not trying to fight him anymore. Whether she just wanted to get her baby out or she'd realized he was trying to help didn't really matter when the end result was the same.

"Last time Otis pulled a calf was the second year I was here." He had his boot heels planted in the earth as he worked. "Dammit. Nearly had it." He was sweating. His still-wet hair fell over his forehead. "Come on, baby. Give me that other hoof." He reached farther, then gave a little shout of triumph. "That's it. That's it. Little farther." She could see him feeding the straps. Knew he was looping the second hoof.

Then he was leaning back, using his weight to help ease one hoof forward, then the other, back and forth, slowly, inexorably walking the calf free. When the mama rested, he took up the slack. When she pushed again, he helped, straining as hard as any man could while helping a female bring her child into the world.

Then the calf finally slid free in a rush and he fell back, too, and yanked his T-shirt over his head to rub it over the slick, black little baby. Rubbing its head. Its face.

"Alive?"

"Yeah."

She hooted and laughed as she sank back on her heels. "Yes!" She grinned at him. "Good job, Dalloway. Hero of the day, here."

He looked up at her and seemed to go still for a moment.

She was flushed. From the heat, from the birth. At least he'd never know the fixed way he was looking at her was making her blush. "Want me to let her loose?"

He finally looked away. "Give me a second." He was still cleaning the calf. Checking its sex. "Got ourselves a little boy." As soon as he said the words, the cow was struggling to her feet. April knew that was a good sign.

"Okay. Let her loose now."

She untied the rope and flipped the loosened loop off the cow's neck. As soon as she did, the mama advanced on Jed and he quickly scooted out of the way so she could bond with her newborn.

He scooped up the straps and his soiled T-shirt. "Toss me that bottle of water, would you?"

She tossed him the water. He poured it over his arms, doing the best he could to clean himself up. She figured unless he stretched out flat in that numbingly cold stream, he wouldn't get much cleaner until he was wedged in the small shower inside his bunkhouse-for-one.

And *that* was an image she needed to get out of her head, pronto. He was already half-naked right in front of her. She didn't need to torment herself even more.

"That was pretty impressive work for a city boy."

He gave her a slanted grin. "If the guys back home only knew just how intimate I've been with a cow." Then he actually gave her a quick wink before he was striding back toward the horses.

She dragged her eyes away from that ogle-worthy sight. A sight only improved because of the stretch of naked male back above his worn leather belt.

"You coming or you just gonna stand there admiring the view?" he called over his shoulder.

She hoped to heaven the view he meant was the one lying beyond the mountain.

But the squiggle inside her said otherwise.

She didn't know if she'd made a mistake coming on this horse ride with him, but for now, she wasn't going to worry about it. There'd be plenty of time to worry about it later.

"The view," she called back to him, unable to stop the laugh that came with it.

Then she jogged after him.

Because, just in case he decided to stretch out flat in that crystal clear stream, she didn't want to miss it.

Chapter Twelve

"What's the word on Snead?"

April clutched her cell phone closer to her ear and stepped out of the kitchen, where Jaimie and Matthew and all of his brothers were grousing about Squire's apparent burst of insanity. "I haven't made any progress, Gage," she admitted when she finally reached the heavy front door and went out onto the porch. "I've tried to catch him at his motel more than once but the guy's slippery."

"Then put on some gloves and catch him."

"Rumor has it he's been talking with a mining company. Someplace out of Ohio. Winemeier Mining. Have you heard of them?"

"Not yet. Call me when you've caught Snead."

He hung up in her ear and she sighed, tapping the phone against her lips before dialing again. This time Snead's motel room. She'd called it so often it was on her frequent numbers.

As usual, he didn't answer. But this time her message was as direct as it could be. Just her name and the dollar figure that Gage was prepared to pay.

If that didn't get a response, she didn't know what would.

From inside the house she could hear her uncles' voices rising then falling as they argued over what should be done about their father and Gloria.

As if there were anything that they *could* do.

She looked at her phone, scrolling through the various images she'd taken of Rambling Mountain and the Rad until she found the one of her grandmother at the library fund-raiser.

Her mom and aunt were rallying around their mother, of course. April had spent nearly an hour on the phone with her mom that morning, listening to her rail about the situation.

To a person, everyone seemed to be blaming Squire.

April was shooting more for impartiality.

She brushed her finger over the photo, then nearly jumped out of her skin when the phone vibrated.

Jed's number replaced the picture of her grandmother laughing up at Tom Hook, and she quickly put the phone to her ear again. "Hi." She cringed at her breathy voice. "Pulled any more calves today?"

"Not so far." He sounded grim. "Heard from the estate administrator. Court has ruled on the succession. Snead's getting everything. Lock, stock and barrel. And he wants everything but the mountain itself sold."

Knowing that it had been coming didn't make it any easier to hear. "I'm sorry, Jed."

"Wanted to let you know. Now's your chance to get out your boss's checkbook."

"Not sure he is going to want to measure his checkbook against a mining company's. Are you okay?"

He was silent for a moment. "Got a copy of the list Eleanor prepared. I need to get the stuff packed up for the auction."

"Some people in your position would just walk away."

"I'm not some people."

How well she knew it. "I'll come and help."

"Why?"

Her hand tightened around the phone. "Because I want to."

"Bring boxes."

She nodded even though he couldn't see it. Even though he'd already hung up.

He was like Gage in that respect.

She returned to the kitchen. The men were still

arguing. Jaimie looked miserable. April leaned over her ear. "I'm going out. If I'm not back later—"

Jaimie patted her hand. "I know. You'll be at Belle's."

April didn't feel like explaining that she was not heading to her aunt's, but to help Jed. "I'll check in with you later."

Instead of heading straight to the Rad, she drove into Weaver first on the hunt for boxes. Stops at Ruby's and Colbys had both her trunk and backseat full up with flattened cardboard boxes. Armed with packing tape and a package of chocolate cookies from Shop-World, she drove back through town again and headed up the mountain.

When she reached the barriers, Jed was already there. Sitting on the tail of the four-wheeler.

Another white T-shirt. Another pair of jeans. His eyes were dark and mesmerizing as he headed her way and she couldn't imagine why she'd ever thought he was anything less than beautiful.

A thought that had her insides swimming more than a little. To combat it, she briskly set her parking brake, popped open her trunk and got out to begin unloading the cartons.

"Strapping tape and chocolate," she told him as he hopped off the UTV. "In the backseat."

"Sounds like a teenage boy's fantasy."

One of the boxes slipped from her grasp and it turned, corner over corner as the wind yanked it back down the road, then sent it toppling right off the edge of the mountain.

She tightened her grip. "Strapping tape," she scoffed. "Hate to be that boy's girlfriend." She brushed past him to make for the UTV.

"More the roses and candlelight type?"

She made herself laugh. "Sure. Why not? With Bollinger Champagne and chocolates purchased firsthand in Belgium." She shoved the boxes in the utility box.

They passed each other again—him with the armload of boxes this time. "Expensive type, are you?"

She spread her arms. "The way my daddy raised me," she lied lightly on her way back to the car. The trunk and backseat were empty. She grabbed the plastic bag from Shop-World, headed back to the utility vehicle and slid onto the seat beside him.

"Ever actually been to Belgium?"

"Ten years ago. High school graduation present. Belgium, Luxembourg, France." She grabbed the seat rail when he started up the engine and rumbled speedily around the boulders. "Two weeks from Bruges to Marseille."

"Fancy gift."

She shrugged. "My parents weren't particularly thrilled, but it was from Alex *Senior*. My dad's father," she elaborated at his look. "They had a rocky relationship. Couldn't agree on anything except for the fact that they couldn't agree on anything. In his will, he stipulated a year abroad for me and any other children my dad might have."

The look she got from him that time was speculative. "A year."

She shrugged. "I didn't spend a year in Europe. I chose two weeks in the fall before I started college and dumped the rest of the money into savings. And—" she lifted her hand "—before any latent investment banker cells come surging to the fore, my dad's advisers took over handling the account years ago. They take care of the trust fund, too."

"Who the hell is your dad?"

She shouldn't have been surprised. It wasn't as if she expected everyone in the known universe to know anything at all about her. It smacked of egotism. "Alex Reed. He founded Huffington—"

"Sports Clinics," he finished. He looked at her as if he'd never seen her before. "He's the guy who took Reed Health Systems public."

"Yeah, so?"

"Made a fortune on that RHS stock."

She made a face. "A lot of people did, evidently."

"So what the hell are you doing tramping around small-town USA trying to cut a deal for a developer when you could be doing just about anything else in the world? *Any*where in the world?"

"Just because I have a healthy trust fund doesn't mean I have any desire to live off it." She waggled the Shop-World bag. "That's not the way I was raised. Everyone in my family knows what the value of a dollar is, because we've always had to earn it. Money is never an indicator of quality or worth. And I like paying my own way, thank you very much."

He shook his head and gunned the engine up the last bit of pavement. "Unbelievable," she heard him mutter before he cut the engine and halted the UTV just shy of the cantilevered deck. He grabbed the entire load of boxes and stomped off.

Irritated, she followed him into the cabin, where he dumped the boxes on the floor. "I don't know what's got you so peeved. It's not like I was hiding anything."

"Before he died, Tanya's father was Chief of Staff at RHS Chicago. And I thought *she* was the boss's daughter."

Her breath exhaled in a whoosh. The universe had a strangely twisted sense of humor. "I'm not *your* boss's daughter, so what are you complaining about?" She pulled the large roll of tape from the bag and grabbed a box from the top of the stack to begin assembling it. "If you want my help packing up the stuff, then get over it and get some scissors or a knife. I forgot to bring one and I can't tear that strapping tape with my teeth."

She preferred the look of annoyance that crossed his face to that stunned look he'd had.

He left the room and she heard him rummaging in the kitchen. He came back with an ancient-looking pair of metal scissors.

Old or not, they'd been kept sharp, and they sliced through the filament tape with ease. With the cardboard once more fashioned into a suitable box, she grabbed it in her hand and stood. "What do I pack and where do I start?"

He produced the copy of Eleanor's list. April gave it a thorough look, and then silently went into Otis's bedroom.

He joined her a few minutes later with another carton and they set to work.

Packing up everything took longer than she expected and with each box that she sealed with the sturdy tape, her thoughts returned to her grandmother and Squire.

They finished the bedroom. Jed left for more than two hours to check the stock while she pulled everything out of a closet, sorting, packing. Discarding very little. It was shocking the variety of items that Eleanor had chosen. Everything from the vintage radio—totally expected—to an ugly smoking pipe. Glassware. Flatware. Boxes of old stamps. Boxes of new stamps.

Jed returned while she was working on the kitchen.

They ran out of boxes and got creative. Using the empty drawers from Otis's dresser. Buckets.

An old laundry basket. All stacking up against one side of the cabin.

Finally, they were finished packing anything that fit in a box, and were sitting in the bare kitchen at the table. A half-empty pack of chocolate sandwich cookies sat between them.

"It's going to take a lot of trips getting all of that down the mountain." Even the furniture, what little there was of it, would be going.

He nodded. Rubbed his hand down his face. "Yep."

She chose another cookie, but held it up, studying the simple perfection of it. "I should have brought milk."

He reached out and snatched the cookie from her fingers, downing it in one bite.

"Hey!" She watched him go to the stack of boxes and drawers and buckets, seeming to look for something.

"Ah." He pulled two glasses from the dish towel they'd been wrapped inside and set them on the table in front of her.

"There's no milk in the fridge," she reminded. "There's nothing in the fridge." She knew. She'd cleaned it out, scouring the shelves and the sides, because it was one more thing that was going to be auctioned.

"Got something better." He disappeared out the back door and returned shortly with a bottle. He unscrewed the cap and tipped it over one glass. Then the other.

"Not Bollinger, but it'll do the job." He set aside the bottle and picked up one glass, clinking the base softly against the rim of the other. "And no. I don't have a drinking problem."

She lifted the glass, sniffed. Took a cautious sip and felt the liquor bloom and warm, heating her throat all the way down. "I thought—"

"I know what you thought." He was studying the contents of his glass. "It was never the alcohol that I craved. I stopped drinking when I came here with Otis. Never found what I wanted in the bottom of a bottle."

She couldn't help but think about the wedding ring he kept with his toothpaste. "W-what did you want?" As if she didn't know.

"An end." His lips twisted. "An end that never came. No matter what I did." He gently swirled the glass. "First day up here, Otis took me up to his ridge. Stood there with me right on the edge of the cliff. Told me if I really wanted to do it, to stop playing at it and do it right. One step and it would all be over."

Her hand trembled and she carefully set her glass back on the table.

"I don't know how many times I made that hike. Stood right there. Toes of my boots hanging an inch over. Wondering why the universe couldn't just make it easy for me. Rockslides happen around here. Small ones. Big ones. You've seen for yourself. But not a single pebble ever slid out from under my feet. Not at that spot." His gaze slid over her. "You believe in God?"

She nodded jerkily. "You?"

"Sadly. The results of a Scotsman father and a Mexican mother." He looked back at his drink. "I finally figured out that neither God nor the Devil wanted me." He stopped swirling the glass and tossed the shot back in one swallow.

"Ever think that God needed you here more? That Otis coming into your life was less happenstance than divine intervention?"

He made a sound. A cross between rusty laugh and something else. "Regardless, here I am."

She knew what he was thinking. That he was here. And Tanya was not. "I should have realized Dalloway was Scottish," she said.

His eyebrow peaked.

"Reed. Go back enough generations it used to be R-E-I-D." She spelled it out.

He made another sound. Less something else. More rusty laugh. "You worried we're cousins or something?"

She picked up the glass again. Took another sip. "And your mom?"

"From Mexico. Crossed the border illegally when she was younger than you were when you were trotting around Belgium. They were both immigrants, but he took the legal route and she didn't. They met working for—"

"Tanya's father," she concluded.

So much for her trying to get him to think of someone else.

"Where my father gardened and my mother cleaned. She was deported when I was nine. I never saw her again."

"Oh, Jed." She couldn't help herself. She caught his hand in hers and squeezed. "I'm so sorry."

He shrugged and reached for the bottle again. Poured another measure for them both, even though she had only taken a few sips. "My dad worked fifteen-hour days making sure I got through school. He never had the means for a proper search for her. Didn't stop him trying. Said he'd love her forever and that's what he did. Cleared my first million when I was twenty-two." He didn't seem to notice her start. "That's when I located her family in Oaxaca. She'd already died. Pneumonia. Dad died a year later. Pretty sure it was a broken heart."

She looked away, dashing a finger under her lashes before she reached for another cookie. She dunked it in the liquor and took a bite. "You're right. Just as good as milk."

He squeezed her hand and let go. "I owe you more than cookies that you brought yourself and a fair-to-middlin' sip of Scotch whisky."

"No you don't."

But he just pulled her out of her chair. "Yes, I do. Dinner at the very least. Steakhouse over in Braden—"

"Good grief, we don't have to drive all the way over to Braden for a decent steak! Colbys is—" She broke off. "Unless you don't want to go somewhere in town. You know. With me."

He gave her a look. "My dad would've called you daft."

Her stomach fluttered. "Let me at least wash up a little. I'm dusty from all the packing."

He waved her off and she quickly went into Otis's bathroom, only to realize she'd forgotten to pack up the cupboard above the washer and dryer. She darted back to the kitchen to grab one of the big black bags they'd been using for the stuff that needed to be hauled off to the trash. "Forgot to empty the stuff over the washer."

"It can wait."

"It'll only take a few minutes, and then it'll be done." She grabbed the copy of Eleanor's list that was sitting on the counter and took it with her.

Jed followed, reaching above her head to pull down the items crammed on the highest shelf. Like her, he set everything on the top of the dryer. "This is all trash. Just hold open the bag." With his arm, he swept everything into the bag.

"Hold on." She rescued an amber-colored ashtray. "It's on the list."

"He was a smoker, that's for sure," Jed muttered. He cleared the next lower shelf. "Always had a pipe stuck in the corner of his mouth when I met him. Didn't stop until last year. Said he wasn't gonna get better, so why stop one of his remaining joys. Only reason he quit was because it hurt too much to continue."

"Not that one, either." She snatched the silver box that had contained the bandages and set it aside. "It's a jewelry box." She looked at the list. "Circa 1800."

He let out a short laugh. "I swear, the only thing that old man didn't keep above the washer and dryer was actual laundry supplies." He tossed her the can of peanut brittle. "Nuts."

She took the can and shook it. Figuring it would rattle. Surprised when it didn't. She turned it upside down. Looked at the lid. "Oh, this is one of those novelty things. You open up the can but instead of the treats, one of those springy snakes flies out." She twisted the top. "See?"

But the snake didn't pop out.

"Terrifying," he said dryly.

"Guess they have a shelf life." She poked her fingertip at the paper curled inside. Then looked more closely and drew it out. It wasn't a snake. It was a small white envelope, yellowing around the edges. Holding a perpetual curl from being stored inside a narrow round can.

"Hold the bag again." He was waiting to push more garbage inside.

"Wait a second." Excitement curled inside her as she slowly uncurled the envelope. There was nothing written on the outside of it, but she knew. She waved it at him and started jumping around like some silly schoolgirl. "This is it! I know it is. Otis's will."

He angled his head closer to her, looking at the envelope. "Nah."

She waved the can at him with its colorful peanut brittle image. "He even told me! Called it his sweet will." She shoved aside all of the stuff on the dryer so she could flatten out the small envelope. "I don't know if we should open it."

"If we don't, how are we going to prove to you that it isn't his will?"

"Don't be such a pessimist." She lifted her head. "We need to call Archer. He'll know what to do."

"The estate's been settled, April."

She swatted him with the envelope. "Well they can *un*settle it!" She closed her hand around his. "Come on. We have to go."

"Thought you wanted to call Archer."

She grabbed her hair in both hands and yanked. "Are you trying to make me crazy?"

His eyes suddenly crinkled. He yanked her

close and pressed a fast kiss on her lips. "Seems fair enough to me," he said when he let her go, just as quickly.

If he noticed that she swayed a little, he didn't say.

"If it *is* his will," he told her over his shoulder, "it doesn't necessarily follow that you'll like what it says. He might not be leaving it to your boss." He snatched up the receiver. "What's the number?"

She went still. "I don't think that. Gage certainly doesn't."

"What about Otis being your boss's father?"

She shook her head. "Gage sounded certain that he wasn't. The only logical person for Otis to leave the ranch to is *you*."

He shook his head. "No. I was only his—"

"—friend." She went over to him, taking his face between her hands. She searched his eyes. "You were his friend. And from everything that I've seen and heard, his *only* friend."

His gaze lowered and her mouth ran dry.

She swallowed and took a step back, holding up Archer's number on her cell phone screen. "What are you waiting for? Start dialing. Probably going to take you at least five minutes on that old rotary dial."

"April."

Her chest felt tight. Her stomach shivery. If anyone else described the feeling, she'd suggest they were coming down with something.

But the only thing she was afflicted with was him.

"Look at it this way. It didn't sound to me like he wanted to leave things to Snead. Now, are you going to call, or do I have to?"

He exhaled sharply.

Then began dialing.

Chapter Thirteen

The envelope *did* contain Otis Lambert's will.

Written out entirely by him. By hand.

It was dated.

It was signed.

But what else it specifically said was going to have to wait.

April sat in the courtroom gallery along with Jed and Archer Templeton while Judge Fernandez conferred with Martin Pastore, who was the lawyer the court had appointed as the estate administrator.

Accompanying Pastore—a middle-aged man who looked to April as if he routinely kicked kittens for entertainment—was a young woman who kept consulting the laptop open in front of her. She wore a severely tailored gray suit that seemed entirely at odds with her riotously curling brown hair.

There were only three rows in the gallery. Wooden benches that seemed more suited to a church than a courtroom, but since April hadn't spent a lot of time in courtrooms, she didn't have a lot of experience to draw upon.

She leaned toward Jed, whispering as if they were in church. "Surprised that Snead isn't here. Do you think he got word?"

"I know he did," Archer assured quietly. He was sitting on the other side of Jed. "Notified him myself when I turned the envelope over to the judge."

That had been Friday.

Now it was Monday afternoon. And the powers that be were trying to decide how to proceed.

The uptight Mr. Pastore strode from the judge's bench back to the table where his associate was busily tapping away on her computer. He bent near her, murmuring something that they couldn't hear, then strode back to talk to the judge again. The curly-haired brunette sneaked a look in their direction, but quickly turned back to her computer when she saw April noticing.

She leaned again. "Archer, they have to accept the will, don't they? Even if Otis did something crazy like leave it all to Dogcatchers of the West?"

"It's a holographic will," Archer murmured. "Entirely handwritten. We just have to prove that it was Otis's hand that did it."

"Otis kept all his books by hand," Jed said. "Only change in the last seventy-some years was when I took over a few years ago." He gestured toward the lawyers. "They've already got the ledgers. Half-dozen boxes worth of proof to match his hand-writing."

"It should be a straightforward matter," Archer agreed. His gaze was following the same path as the brunette with the computer. Going from the courtroom doorway and back again. "Who's Nell watching for?" he wondered aloud.

"You know her?"

"You might say that. Cornelia Brewster." He looked like he'd swallowed something bitter. "My stepsister's best friend."

April leaned forward. Lowered her voice again. "This isn't a conflict of interest, right?"

Irony shoved aside the bitter as he smiled. "Plenty of conflict, doll, but not in this situation."

She rolled her eyes. "Don't call me doll."

"It's so much fun to yank her chain," Archer said to Jed. "Oh, *hello*." The courtroom doors had flown open and Snead walked in, strutting like he was very much lord of the manor.

The overlong hair had been groomed. The mustache tamed.

Gone was the vile green suit. In its place was a

charcoal gray one that smacked of being custom-made. She knew. Her father had a preference for them.

She realized she far preferred Jed's style. Clean jeans. White button-down shirt. He'd tucked it in this time, in deference to the courthouse.

Jed leaned close to her ear. "He still looks like a ferret."

She closed her hand over his. She agreed. But she was less concerned with Louis Snead's new uptown look than she was with the entourage following him into the courtroom.

And Archer's grimace didn't help any.

Snead and his party arranged themselves across from them in the gallery and Pastore headed back to his table. He didn't seem surprised by the late arrivals. But then he'd probably had plenty of dealings with Snead already. He sat down beside Cornelia. The brunette didn't send Archer any more sideways looks. Nor did she keep looking toward the door.

The ones she'd been watching for had arrived.

Judge Fernandez was an unsmiling woman whom April didn't know. She was from the district court, and Archer had told her and Jed they were lucky to slip into the docket last minute since she traveled among several municipalities. From Weaver or not, she at least didn't seem particularly delighted by the latecomers. "We're not turning this into a circus," she warned before calling the session to order. "It's already quitting time, and I want to keep this brief. We're here today for one purpose only. This." She lifted a clear bag containing the familiar yellowing envelope between her fingers. "While it appears this document is the last will and testament of Otis Jerome Lambert, the estate in question is obviously one of significant importance. Therefore, I'm going to allow a reasonable period for proof."

Snead jumped to his feet, despite the tugging on his sleeves he earned from his companions. "Your Honor, I've already been recognized as my dear cousin's only heir. That man—" he pointed toward Jed "—had undue influence over Otis. We're supposed to believe he only just now found the will? I don't—"

The judge gave him an annoyed glare. "Sit down, Mr. Snead. I'm well aware that until his death, you had no interactions with your dear cousin whatsoever. This is not a hearing for you to air your opinions."

He grudgingly sat.

"Mr. Pastore." Judge Fernandez looked over her rimless glasses at the attorney. "You will work out a time for our next meeting with my clerk at which point I'll rule on the validity of the will. Two weeks from now should be sufficient to work into the schedule." She lifted her palm toward Snead's direction. "And before you bother again, your opinion on the matter is noted for the court."

"Two weeks!" Snead hopped up again despite her warning. "I can't wait that long. I have a right to know what it says!"

"Mr. Snead, you can wait as long as I say you can wait and so can your new friends there from Winemeier Mining. I know you're all salivating over the prospect of mining Rambling Mountain."

"Your Honor." Mr. Pastore popped out of his seat. "With respect, Mr. Snead's business interests are hardly relevant."

"That's right!" Snead shouted. "What I do with my land is my business!"

The judge sent them all a quelling look. "And if you interrupt one more time, I'll hold you in contempt." Her eyes swept across the room. "If or when the document is proven, it will be entered and the contents will become public record. Adjourned." She slapped her gavel, rose from the bench and strode out of the room.

"And the games will begin," Archer murmured. He gestured and they followed him from the courtroom, past Snead, who was huddled with his entourage, waving his arms around and looking frantic.

As the double doors swung closed behind them, April saw Pastore approaching Snead's trio.

"Mr. Pastore doesn't have anything to gain, does he? Regardless of what happens with the will?"

"I have no love for Martin Pastore," Archer admitted, "but even he has some respect for the rule of law." He gave them an encouraging smile. "Keep in mind that the judge could have denied the will out of hand, but she didn't. Now, we just need to make sure the thing is deemed valid."

"It's certainly not fraudulent," April said quickly.

"I know," Archer soothed. "This is just going to add to the length of the probate, which never moves quickly anyway."

"So what is Jed supposed to do in the meantime?"

"Continue following the stipulations that Pastore has already assigned where the ranch is concerned. It's not to anyone's benefit that the livestock suffers or the ranch falls into disrepair." He eyed Jed. "I know you're receiving compensation for your caretaking duties, but you do have a choice."

Jed's eyes slid toward Snead. His lips twisted. "Do I?"

"So now what?"

They'd parted company with Archer at the courthouse and somehow ended up walking to the park. To the gazebo.

It was a late Monday afternoon. They could hear the children from the schoolyard not far away, where a baseball game was in full play. The park itself, though, was quiet.

April chewed the inside of her cheek, studying Jed's face. "Well? Now what? Archer *was* right. I know you don't necessarily agree, but you really do have a choice. You don't have to keep working the Rad."

"Who else is going to? I promised Otis." He sat down on the edge of the raised deck of the gazebo. "This thing needs to be painted."

"Winters are hard on it. It probably needs painting every year. Pastore could hire someone else to tend the stock."

"Leaving me to take your uncle's offer? Work at the Double-C?"

"That's not what I meant." She sat beside him. He was right. When she closed her hand over the wood beside her, the paint was chipping and ragged. "In a few weeks, when Otis's will is accepted—"

"—I'll need to find work. If not there, then somewhere else. And the days of me working in finance are done."

It shook her to think that he might leave Weaver. "B-because you're not interested in finance anymore?"

His lips twisted. "Because *it* isn't interested in me."

"I don't understand."

His arm brushed hers when he gripped the edge of the wood the same way she was. "The firm I worked for was Hampton-Tiggs."

Even though she tried, she couldn't squelch her shock.

And he obviously recognized it.

"Yeah." He gave her one look and grimaced. "*That* Hampton-Tiggs."

The once-prestigious financial institution had made the news all around the country when the company's two principals—Macarthur Hampton and Veronica Tiggs—were arrested for fraud, theft and money laundering. "I was in college when all that hit. Nearly ten years ago, wasn't it?"

"Eight." He looked her way again. "Go ahead and ask. Everyone else did."

"Sorry?"

"If I knew." His lips thinned. "I didn't. A lot of us didn't. But it took a six-month criminal investigation to convince anyone. Didn't matter that we were cleared. Guilt by association was enough to end a lot of careers. Not just mine."

Eight years ago. He'd told her his wife had died eight years ago, too. She couldn't help wondering if it had been before or after.

But what did it matter, anyway?

She looked down. They were both cupping the edge of the wood. Only a few inches separated her hand from his.

She stretched out her pinkie finger and touched him. "I'm sorry. That was a really awful year for you." Followed by several more. Before he and Otis had encountered one another. "What happened to the others?"

"No idea. There's some bull notion that people going through the same crisis will band together. But they don't. We spent eighty-hour weeks working together, but when the scandal hit, we couldn't get away from each other fast enough. Rats on a sinking ship."

"Hardly rats. You just said you didn't know what was happening."

"Should have. Right under our noses."

"I think you're too hard on yourself. And before you start to argue with me, you keep making assumptions about what Otis wrote in his will."

"And you don't?"

She had to give him that point. "Well, it's only two weeks and you'll know." She hopped down and dusted her hands together. "We'll all know. You have only one thing you have to decide right now."

"What's that?"

"Where you're taking me for that steak you promised me."

"That was three days ago."

She lifted her hands. "A promise is a promise."

His gaze ran from her head to her toes and back up again. Unlike Jed, she had worn a suit to court. "You're overdressed for Colbys."

The warmth running inside her had nothing to do with the warm day and everything to do with that look of his. She slipped out of her suit jacket, leaving the black slacks and thin gray tank. "Better?"

He shook his head regretfully. "Still over-dressed."

She huffed and looked down at herself. There was no regular dress code at Colbys. Pretty much anything went, as long as it included clothing. "I am not."

His eyes suddenly glinted. "For what I have in mind?"

Shivers skidded along her spine. Somehow, she managed to ignore them and gave him a smirk. "Tempting as you think that might be, let's just stick to being friends."

A smile was flirting around the corners of his mouth, making that little scar look more like a dimple. "Friends can—"

"*Clothed* friends," she said blithely. "Not that you're not…sort of cute and all." A description for him that couldn't have been further from the truth. Jed Dalloway was definitely attractive. But most definitely not in a cute, harmless sort of way. "Nevertheless, you know, better that we don't—" She waved her hand. "You know."

He stood, too. Sort of rose up, like a lion who was leisurely waking up from a nap in the sun. "You know?"

Her mouth felt dry. She took a step back, only to feel her high heel sink into the grass. She wobbled slightly, adjusting her footing. "Don't play dumb."

His hand clasped her arm. "You don't seem real steady there."

"It's the grass." She tugged her arm free. "I can be your friend, Jed. But I...I can't be your friend with benefits. I'm not made that way."

His eyes narrowed slightly. "I see."

"Do you?" She stepped back again. Sank into the grass again and heaved out a sigh. "Wish I did," she muttered, finally just stepping out of the high-heeled pumps and leaning down to pull them free from the grass.

"You're not in Weaver for the long haul."

She straightened slowly.

"You're here because of Rambling Mountain."

What he was saying was true. And so, so far from the truth.

She dangled her shoes from her fingers. She was tired of talking about the matter. No matter what happened with the will, she felt certain her boss was destined for disappointment, and she was hard-pressed to feel regret. Not when she felt so strongly that Otis would have left everything to Jed. "Where's that steak?"

His dark eyes studied her for a moment. Then his head dipped slightly and he gestured. "Across the street."

She forced a friendly smile and started off across the grass in her bare feet.

After a moment, he followed. When she reached

the sidewalk, she stopped to slip on her shoes once more, and then they crossed the street, aiming for the grill.

The place wasn't quite as busy as it usually was, and they took a small high-top table near the window overlooking the street. April hung her jacket over the back of her chair when Jed pulled it out for her before sitting. When they were both seated, his knees brushed against hers.

"Sorry," he murmured.

Privately, she didn't think he really looked it and she was painfully grateful when a perky-faced waitress came by to deliver tall glasses of ice water.

"Special from the grill tonight is lasagna." The waitress handed them their menus. "Get you started on something from the bar?"

April shook her head. The last thing she needed was alcohol. "Just the water, thanks." She set aside the menu without needing to even open it. "I'll have the rib eye. Medium rare. No onions or mushrooms. Baked potato with all the fixings."

"Same," Jed said when the waitress turned her attention to him. He shifted in his seat, glancing toward the bar and his knee brushed April's again. "Plus whatever seasonal you have on tap."

"You bet." The waitress scooped up the unnecessary menus and headed off.

His knee was still pressed against April's.

She lifted her water and took a long drink, but it did little to calm the rattling going on inside her.

"So what do you hear from Loverboy?"

She nearly choked on the water and quickly set it aside. "Kenneth?"

"You have more than one lover boy?"

"He's not my lover boy. He never was. And I haven't seen him since, well, you know."

"Not even when you went back to Denver?"

"Not even."

The waitress returned with Jed's frosty glass of beer and when she left again, April rested her forearms on the table, clasping her hands together. "How old are you?"

His brows quirked. "Why?"

She shrugged. "Curious."

"Thirty-two."

She hid her shock. He looked older. Considering everything he'd gone through, she shouldn't have felt so surprised. He'd lost his wife and his career eight years ago. Which meant he'd been just twenty-four.

"You're still young," she said. "When the Rad is yours, is that how you want to live out your life? Ranching the hard way on the side of a mountain?"

"It won't end up mine."

"*Why* are you so certain of that? I would have sworn that you loved the ranch. Loved the mountain itself. Do you just not want it?"

"Nothing I've ever loved has lasted."

An ache filled her chest. "That doesn't mean this wouldn't. You told me you believed the mountain should be shared. You could retain the ranch. Sell the rest."

"To your boss."

"Well, certainly not to Winemeier Mining!"

"Is that what this has all been about?"

"What do you mean?"

"Hedging your bets? The whole *friend* routine? Just in case that old man leaves me the mountain?"

"Wow." Stung, she sat back and had to fight the urge to get up and walk away. "That came out of left field. You really are cynical."

"Realistic. You're here to strike a deal. With someone. You wouldn't be the first woman to sleep—"

Fire shot through her veins, incinerating anything as mild as *stung*. "Don't even go there," she cut him off. "I didn't sleep with you for a bloody deal. I slept with you because I—" She managed to put the skids on her hot tongue and slid off the stool. "You know what? If you know me so little by now, it doesn't even matter."

She grabbed her jacket and spun on her heel. She'd never seen red before. But she saw it now. It actually hazed her vision as she strode toward the exit and shoved through the door so hard it bounced back against the wall.

Outside on the sidewalk, she immediately turned and kept right on walking, her heels snapping out angrily on the cement.

She'd reached the end of the block before she even realized it. Her car was still parked at the courthouse. In the opposite direction.

She cursed under her breath and turned around to start walking back. Her ears were still buzzing. "Impossible. Impossible—" She couldn't think of a word vilifying enough. *"Man."*

"Whoa there, doll."

She glared up at Archer. "Where the hell did you come from?"

"Sheriff's Office."

It was almost directly across the street.

"What's got you in such a lather?"

"Who says I'm in a lather?"

His hands went up peaceably. "The snarl?"

"Well, I have a whole lot more where they come from," she assured, and stepped around him. "And don't call me *doll*!"

Through the window, Jed watched April stomp across the street. Her long red hair was bouncing against her back. Less than a minute later, Archer Templeton had pushed through the door of Colbys and his gaze landed on Jed.

The other man looked wryly amused as he approached. "Where's the date?" He nodded toward the two steak dinners on the table.

"On her way back to Denver, no doubt."

"A certain testy redhead?"

"She's not testy. She's just facing reality." Jed gestured with his empty glass. "Want a steak?"

Archer pulled out the chair, angling it so he had more legroom. "Looks as excellent as the steaks always are here, but I'll pass."

He gestured to the waitress and pointed at Jed's beer. He held up two fingers.

She nodded and headed to the bar.

"Doesn't look like you're in the mood to eat, either," the other man pointed out. "What reality?"

"Once a bastard, always a bastard."

"Speaking personally, or about our friend Snead?"

"Either applies."

The cheerful waitress veered to their table, delivered the drinks and after learning that Archer didn't want a menu, headed off again.

"Pretty girl," the lawyer commented.

"Didn't notice." Jed stabbed at his steak once and set down his fork. He picked up the fresh beer, but didn't drink that, either.

"You should go after her."

Jed knew the guy didn't mean the waitress.

"That's an attorney for you. Always handing out the advice." He waited a beat. "Wanted or not."

Archer smiled faintly. "We have that tendency." He took a long drink. "Too bad I never take my own." He looked back at Jed. "I know who you are. John Edward Dalloway."

Jed went still. He looked past the attorney, out the window. Seeing the past more than the street outside. It was like looking down a long hallway. One that didn't hold the pain that it once did, but one that would always be there. Reminding him.

"That was a long time ago," he said finally.

The other man was drumming the table in a deceptively leisurely way. "Not going to ask why I know who you are?"

Jed toyed with the beer. "You're representing her boss. The developer. Pays to know who all the players are at the table."

"Are you *at* the table?"

Jed grimaced. "Not by choice. None of us knows what that will contains yet, but it would have been easier if April hadn't found it."

"Even though it would have meant Snead getting it all."

"He still might."

"True."

"She'll be able to keep him from selling to the mining company."

"How do you know?" Archer raised an eyebrow.

"You're not the only one who can do his research. Winemeier isn't as stable as they appear." He saw the glint in the attorney's eyes. "Surprise, surprise."

Archer sat forward, resting his arms on the table. "Neither is Snead. He's in debt up to his eyeballs."

"Not like Winemeier is. Family owned. And there's a power struggle going on between them all. They'll take too long structuring the deal. Stanton just needs to move quickly."

Archer looked curious. "Aside from wondering how you know all that—"

"Library has adequate internet."

He smiled. "Not according to my grandmother, Vivian." Then his smile died, but evidently his curiosity didn't. "Most people wouldn't give away a second chance at a fortune. But it sounds like you might."

"You know who I am, then you know the first fortune didn't get me anywhere."

"I know you didn't have to give yours away to put into a fund benefitting the victims of Hampton-Tiggs."

"On that, you and my late wife would have agreed." Jed pulled out his worn leather wallet and extracted enough cash for the untouched meals plus tip. "Otis didn't want his land going to a developer.

April's best chance of getting her deal is with Snead." He tossed the cash on the table and stood. "Or anyone else, for that matter. Anyone other than me."

Chapter Fourteen

"I think you should stay."

April looked away from her grandmother's concerned face, pretending an interest in the scrambled eggs on her plate. "I need to get back to Denver. Toss out the houseplants I've left dying."

Belle refilled April's coffee cup, then sat down at the table and tucked her dark hair behind her ear. "What about Lambert's will?"

April continued rearranging her eggs. Rather than return to the Double-C after she'd walked out on Jed the previous day, she'd gone to her aunt and uncle's ranch. Mostly because she'd gained a painful understanding for her grandmother making that stand against Squire.

She was as furious with Jed over his insinuation as she'd ever been in her life, and they'd only known one another a matter of months.

What was it like for Gloria? She'd married Squire when April's mom and aunt were just teenagers. Shouldn't a couple be safe after so long together?

She realized her aunt was still waiting for an answer and lifted her shoulder. "The judge said she'll rule in a couple weeks. If Gage wants to pursue it then, that'll be his choice. For me, I'm done. He doesn't need me to make this deal." She gave up on the eggs and lifted her cup, burying her nose in it.

"I still think you should stay," Gloria repeated. She rose and tightened the belt on her flowered robe before she whisked away April's nearly untouched plate. "And not because of Rambling Mountain." She scraped the plate into the trash. "Your breakfast has been cold for an hour."

"I guess I wasn't hungry."

She saw the look that passed between her aunt and grandmother.

"You're always hungry," Belle pointed out gently, as if it were stunning news. "What about Jed?"

April's throat tightened. "What about him?"

Again, a look passed between Belle and Gloria.

"Honey…" Gloria sounded vaguely chiding. "One look at your face tells us how much you care for him. You're in love with him."

"You can't love someone you've barely met two months ago."

Her aunt and grandmother gave her twin looks of "are you kidding me?"

Gloria was the first to speak. "Sweetheart, I fell in love with Squire two hours into meeting that damn man. Not that I was going to admit it to him, of course."

"And here you are." April waved her hand, encompassing Belle and Cage's kitchen at the Lazy-B.

"That is because your grandfather needs to get his head out of his hind end. Not because I don't still love him. Instead of living in the here and now, he's twisting about something that happened long ago when he was just a young man."

She snatched up the bowl that had held the scrambled eggs and went back to the sink. But April had seen the way Gloria's eyes glistened, which was an alarming rarity.

Dishes clattered in the sink. "He's not a young man now. Not even a middle-aged one, despite what he may think inside that hard head of his." She sniffed. "I'm well aware that Sarah was the love of his life, but I have stood by him and been his partner for more than thirty years. I don't think it's too much to want him enjoying *our* life and the time we have left without him always getting sidetracked about the distant past."

Belle looked like she was ready to cry. She got up

and went to her mother, hugging her. April wiped her eyes with her crumpled napkin.

"I loved your daddy, Belle," Gloria choked. "But—" She broke off.

"I know, Mom. It's all right. You and Squire are meant to be together." Belle lifted her head and gave April a wet wink. "He'll come to his senses and show up here to haul you right back where you belong," she assured bracingly. "You know he will."

Gloria made a sound, half-tearful, half-wry. "Yes, well, frankly, I wish he'd get on about it before I lose my willpower and just go on home, myself." She patted her daughter's shoulder, dashed her cheek and tightened her robe again, once more in control, even though her eyes still looked damp.

She moved briskly back to the table to clear a few more plates. "Good lesson to learn, April." She gave her a direct look. "Age doesn't matter a speck when it comes to love." She pointed toward her with the stack of plates. "You love that man. Or you'd have negotiated a deal with that Snead fellow as soon as the wind turned his direction weeks ago, instead of hanging around helping Jed. Finding that will."

"Finding the will was an accident. Turning it in was the right thing to do."

"Of course it was. And I still think you should stay."

"For what?" She shoved her chair back and stood. "He accused me of sleeping with him over *business*!"

Her cheeks heated at the admission but she was too far gone to care. "He does not know me at all. And why would he care to? He's not over his wife. And I must've missed inheriting that strong gene of yours, Grandma. This isn't like you and Squire back in the day. I can't hang around here, hoping that one day he'll want to move on, or that when that day comes, he'll want to move on with *me*."

"Because your life in Denver is so perfect?"

"Because it hurts too much!"

Gloria's eyes softened. "Well, at least you're admitting it."

The pressure in her chest grew. "Yes, well, I'll get over it." If she said it often enough, maybe there was an actual chance of it one day coming true.

"Are you sure you want to?"

She pressed her fingertips to the pain in her forehead. "I told you. He's not over his wife. Frankly, I don't think he ever will be."

"He's told you that?"

"Some things don't have to be said." And the thing that he *had* said was going to burn inside her for a good long while. Because her chest felt like a vise was squeezing it, she pushed away from the table. "I need to go back to the big house and get my things."

"Are you going to see Piper before you go?"

April felt an entirely different stab. She hadn't talked with her friend even once since coming back to Weaver. "She's at school." She brushed a kiss over her aunt's cheek. "Thanks for letting me crash. And tell Cage thanks for the loan." She plucked at the oversize black T-shirt she'd slept in. She knew he'd been out working cattle since dawn.

"You could stay and tell him yourself. He'll be in for lunch in a few hours."

She knew what Belle was trying to do. Thinking if April stayed a little longer, the two of them would convince her not to go. They'd probably get her mom on the phone, too, so that Nikki could add her well-intended pressure. "It's a long drive back to Denver." Her throat was tight. She gave her grandmother a hug. "Love you."

Gloria squeezed her. "Will you still come back for the barbecue next week on Memorial Day?"

Every year the Double-C hosted a huge barbecue for the holiday. April usually tried to make it. "We'll see." She straightened and gave her grandmother a close look. "Will you?"

Gloria's lips lifted slightly. "We'll see," she returned. "Squire will miss you terribly if you don't."

"Play dirty, why don't you?"

Gloria's smile grew. "We use what tools we have." She patted April's shoulder. "It's okay, sweetheart. You do what you need to do. As long as you stay honest with yourself."

On that oh-so-delightful note, April slunk back

to the guest room and changed once more into her clothes from the day before.

Turmoil whirled in her head as she drove back to the ranch.

The house was empty when she got there, which was some small relief, since it meant not having to explain herself to anyone else. She showered quickly, and then packed up. She hadn't brought a lot of clothes with her, so it didn't take long. She left a note on the kitchen table that she'd gone back to Denver and went out to her car.

Try as she might, she couldn't stop herself from looking toward Rambling Mountain. From imagining Jed and Rufus picking their way from that weathered shack down to that creek-side meadow.

The acute ache inside her was still mired in fury. So much so that she still couldn't tell which was worse.

Get over it, April.

She tossed her suitcase into the trunk, slammed it shut loudly and got behind the wheel. "You'll be home by supper," she told herself as she drove away from the big house.

A combine was lumbering down the highway when she reached it and she waited for it to pass. Her gaze kept straying to the mountain.

"Hurry up," she muttered to the tractor. Which was about as effective as spitting into the wind.

Finally, it was past and she pulled out onto the highway, the mountain in her rearview mirror.

She made it nearly to Weaver, before she suddenly pulled around in a U-turn and started back. Her pulse thrumming in her ears, she drove past the ranch entrance. Caught up to the combine and passed it, too, while the mountain loomed larger and larger until she turned off onto the private road that wound its way up the side. The pickup truck was gone when she finally reached the barricades and the UTV was parked on the other side of the boulders.

Jed wasn't there. And that was just as well.

She pulled out her pen and quickly scrawled on the back of a business card. Then she walked up the rest of the way, bypassed the weathered cabin, and pushed open the door of Jed's bunkhouse. She already knew it had no lock.

She didn't linger. Didn't want to allow the sight of the plaid blanket on the bed to remind her. She placed the business card squarely on the top of the blanket and turned around.

Samson was sitting in the doorway, flopping his tail. The teeth that could look so ferocious now curved as if in a happy grin.

She crouched down next to the dog and wrapped her arms around his neck. "Take care of him," she said against that thick gray hair.

Then she stood and walked away.

Not even the constant wind was enough to dry her cheeks.

* * *

Muddy and tired from a day of wrangling cows for a man who wasn't even around anymore to care, Jed let himself and Samson into the bunkhouse.

He noticed the small white rectangle sitting on his bed almost immediately and knew in his bones that it was from April.

He gave the bed as wide a berth as the dinky place allowed and threw off his filthy clothes in the bathroom. "Come on, dog."

Samson whined. But he was as muddy as Jed was and finally the dog stepped under the shower that Jed didn't bother trying to heat.

He scrubbed over the dog until he was clean enough to let run free and then he just stood there alone, head bowed under the beat of the icy spray until the water pooling around his feet ran clear.

He shut off the water. Got out and sluiced the moisture from his face and raked his hair out of his eyes with his fingers. His grim face stared back at him from the mirror on the medicine chest and he yanked it open, pulling out the bottle of aspirin. He swallowed one dry, then went out to pick up the business card she'd left.

The message was brief. Written in the same neatly slanting hand that had graced her note for Otis that first day.

A dollar sign. Followed by a whole lot of commas and zeros and the words "Top offer."

It was a helluva lot of money. But not as much as he knew the land was really worth.

The aspirin was stuck somewhere midway down. He rubbed the pain it was causing in his chest and set the card, dollar signs and zeros facing down, on the counter.

When Samson suddenly stopped trying to shake his coat dry and growled softly, Jed's nerves tightened all over again.

The dog took off like a shot when Jed opened the door. He followed more slowly after dashing himself with a towel and yanking on his jeans and boots.

The cause of the growl was apparent as soon as Jed rounded the cabin.

Samson was on his haunches, teeth bared.

Jed knew it wasn't the horse that had the dog's hair standing up, but the rider.

He finished pulling on the shirt he'd grabbed and eyed the man. Below the tan Stetson was a shock of iron-gray hair. Below that, a steady look from blue eyes so pale they seemed almost white.

If Squire Clay was wary about the hackles Samson was displaying, it didn't show.

"You ride all the way up here from the Double-C, Mr. Clay?" It would have taken him half the day or more.

His visitor's lined face creased even more. "Not the first time I've done it. But no. Left the trailer about ten miles down the hill." Squire's uncompromising gaze switched from Jed's face to look up at the cabin, then out over the view. "Every ten years or so, I'd come up here, trying to deal with Lambert. He ever tell you that?"

Jed smiled slightly. "A time or two."

The elderly man grunted. "Easier coming up on horseback than having to walk that last stretch of road after the slide. Might need to bury me, too, if I tried." He nudged his hat back a few inches and rested his crossed wrists on the saddle horn. "Any news about that will?"

Jed shook his head. "Not yet."

Squire sucked air between his teeth. His saddle creaked softly again.

"Nice-looking horse."

The old man nodded and ran a hand over the palomino's neck. "Clays breed some mighty fine horses. My son tells me you turned him down on the job."

Jed nodded once. He wasn't inclined to explain himself.

Squire crossed his wrists again. "Figure my chances of getting those acres I want are dwindling by the day. But the offer still stands. Fair market value."

"You should be telling that to Snead."

"I 'spect I'll be talking with that twit before long."

Jed considered *twit* a mild term where Snead was

concerned. "Thought you wouldn't try to negotiate against your granddaughter."

"She's gone."

Knowing it would happen didn't stop his stomach from turning hollow.

"Since I'm up here, might as well tell you that I have a fair interest in the herd, too." He squinted off into the distance. "Figure Lambert's rolling around in his grave now, laughin' hard about me admitting it. He and I never did see much eye to eye."

Jed couldn't deny that. "Otis is probably laughing about a hell of a lot these days."

Squire harrumphed. "He did like spiking people's guns."

"Pretty certain he's not the only one."

Squire gave a sharp crack of laughter and a herd of wrens shot from the grass into the air. "True enough." He looked out beyond the cliffs. "Always was a damn pretty view up here. Been in this land as long as Otis was. I started with nothing. He started with a mountain."

"Now you have one of the most profitable cattle companies in the western United States. And the Rad probably hasn't changed in the last fifty years."

"I know you started with nothing, too."

Jed listened to the buzz of insects. Felt the breeze pull at his shirt. For five years, he'd lived there with nobody but Otis knowing his past. Now, in the span of two days, it'd turned into a trending topic. He kept his voice expressionless. "Thought you and Otis weren't on that good of terms."

"Otis didn't say squat. But you've been keeping company with my granddaughter. And I make it a point to know the company my family's keeping."

She's not keeping company here when she's gone back to her life in Denver. He kept the thought to himself. "Is that the real reason you came up here? To tell me I'm not good enough for her?"

"Are you?"

"No."

Squire settled his hat more squarely on his head. "I wasn't good enough for my wife, either."

"Which one?"

A corner of his stern lips lifted. "Both." Then he thumbed his hat back an inch again and leaned forward. His gaze was penetrating. "But a man changes, son. When he finds a treasure worth it."

"Man still has to have something to offer. And I've got as much nothing now as I ever had." He regretted the admission, even though he figured it was an obvious one. "I'll convey your interest to Martin Pastore," he said abruptly. "He's the one in charge of the estate."

"Lawyers." Squire's lip curled almost as much as it had when he'd mentioned Snead. "Heard of Pastore. Usually sticks down in Cheyenne." He waved an all-encompassing arm. "Figures he'd get himself involved in a thing like this." His gaze sharpened on Jed again as he gathered up his reins. "You think about what I said."

"I'm not the one to talk to about a deal, Mr. Clay."

"Wasn't talking about the mountain," Squire said evenly. "Mind if I give Birdie here a water before I head back? I know where the trough is."

In answer, Jed shoved his hands down his front pockets and turned sideways.

Squire clucked softly and the horse swished her white-blond tail and angled beyond the cabin.

Jed was still standing there when they reappeared a short while later. Squire nodded his head once as he passed and Jed watched him ride away.

When the soft clip-clop of hooves on rough road finally faded away, he went to the cabin.

The boxes that April had helped him pack were still sitting there. Finding the will had put a halt on everything, including sending it all off to the auction house. He walked through to the bathroom and grabbed his clothes out of the dryer.

If he'd had a choice, he wouldn't go in the cabin at all. But he had to get his clothes clean somehow.

Bunching everything under one arm, he went out through the kitchen.

The bottle of scotch was still sitting on the table, where it had been since the day she'd helped him pack.

In his bunkhouse, he dumped the clothes on a

chair, then went out and filled a bucket with water and trudged it on foot all the way up to Otis's ridge.

He dumped the water over the riotous flowers then turned his gaze out.

"Gonna miss this place, Otis." The knowledge sat under his breastbone, a deeper ache than he ever would have expected. It provided a good strong base for the slice he felt whenever he thought about April. "I'm doing what I can for you. And for this place. But day's going to be here before long when I won't have that choice anymore. Figure you knew that, though."

He dropped his boot on the bucket to keep it from blowing away. "Don't know where things'll take me." Streaming red hair and a fluttering yellow dress swam in his mind and he closed it off, but not well enough to stop the throb of missing her. "Just know it won't be like before, when you pulled me up. God knows why I'm still on this earth, but I'll stick around until he's done with me. Know that's not something you ever concerned yourself with too much." He studied the flat headstone. "If I was here, I was here. If I decided to step off the cliff, you'd have kept right on being the same as ever."

His shirt flapped. The flowers bobbed and swayed.

Some things stayed constant.

The mountain. The wind.

The fact that Tanya's last words to him still applied.

What is the point of you?

He leaned over to grab the bucket handle. Briefly pressed his hand against the marker. "Rest easy, old man."

Then he straightened and went back down to the bunkhouse that was still his home.

At least for the next few weeks.

Chapter Fifteen

"**Q**uite a crowd," Gage said two weeks later when he and April arrived at the Weaver courthouse.

They'd flown up from Denver by charter that morning, making quick work of the trip, even including flying over Rambling Mountain. It was handy that April's uncle Tristan happened to have a private airstrip outside of town. Gage's ex-wife, Jane, had arranged an SUV to be there waiting for their use.

"Mmm." Even though she'd spent the past three days—ever since they'd gotten word from Archer about the court schedule—mentally girding herself, she couldn't stop searching the people gathered there for Jed.

But she didn't see him.

Pastore and his associate were there. Snead, of course. Wearing one of his uptown suits, though it looked to her like it was hanging on his skinnier-than-ever frame, and the entourage who'd accompanied him last time was missing. She saw the mayor, who did have an entourage. A suited woman she recognized from the state Senate. Even Vivian Templeton's chatty assistant, who'd taken Gage's check that day.

"Sure you want to do this?" Gage asked. "You're really willing to invest your trust fund?"

They'd had the conversation more than once. Ever since she'd proposed the idea of adding her trust fund to his investment and becoming a silent, minority partner. "If the will's not accepted, together we'll be able to outbid Winemeier for certain." They knew it for a fact, since Archer had managed to find out just how deep the mining company's pockets actually were.

"If the will is accepted?"

"Then it's moot, because Jed'll inherit."

"Nobody knows that, yet," Gage cautioned.

"Then you'll get the mountain from whoever does." She spotted Squire about the same time he spotted her and waved. "There's my grandfather, so remember all that is just between you and me." Despite what Gloria had said that day at the Lazy-B, she was still staying there. Still hadn't returned to the Double-C. June had arrived and Squire wasn't hauling, nor was Gloria returning under her own steam. "I'll introduce you."

"Look a lot like your mama," Squire greeted as he leaned down to give her a hug. "She always used to wear suits like this when she was working for your dad."

April smiled and gestured. "This is my boss, Gage Stanton. Gage, my grandfather, Squire Clay."

Squire shifted his walking stick to his other hand in order to shake Gage's hand. "Lot of curious folks turning out today," he observed. "There's not a room *in* this courthouse big enough to fit 'em all."

Gage was just as tall as Squire. Black-haired against iron-gray. "You here as a council member or because of your own interest?"

Squire gave a chuckle. "Both. They're gonna have a stampede on their hands if they don't open the courtroom door soon."

"Archer's here," April said, watching the attorney work his way toward them. If she'd expected Jed to be with him for some reason, she would have been disappointed again.

"Place is a zoo," the attorney said when he reached them. He gave a nod toward Squire. "Good to see you."

Fortunately, despite Squire's antipathy toward Vivian, he didn't extend it to her grandchildren and he returned the greeting in a friendly enough way.

"Any luck finding out how she intends to rule?"

Archer shook his head at Gage's question. "Not even Pastore knows." His gaze strayed toward the opposing team. "At least that's what Nell told me yesterday. If it's true, at least we're all in the same boat."

The courtroom doors swung open as he spoke, and the crowd surged inside. She wasn't sure if it was simply determination or some well-placed blocks by Squire's walking stick, but the four of them managed to get a place in the front row of the gallery. Unfortunately, Louis Snead also slid in next to her, taking up the last of the space.

"Thought about raising that top offer?"

She had to work hard not to shudder. The man was positively oily. "We can discuss that if there turns out to actually be a reason to discuss it with *you*."

"I'm confident."

The chewed-off nails on his fingers implied otherwise. Either that or he had a terrifically bad habit.

She couldn't help herself. She looked over her shoulder. Scanned the faces in the gallery seats. The ones crowded behind them. The senator was directly behind Squire and kept leaning forward over his shoulder to talk to him.

April faced forward again to see the judge had entered the courtroom and was now sitting behind the bench.

"Standing room only," Squire murmured across Gage. "Figured I'd see Jed here."

She didn't reply. So had she.

The hearing was called to order and the judge looked over the top of her glasses. "This will be brief, and since we have a few more laypeople here than usual—" her dry statement earned a smattering of laughter "—I'll speak plainly. The holographic will dated November 2 of last year written by Otis Lambert has been duly authenticated—" she raised her voice over the swell of comments, including the noisy cursing coming from Snead "—to the court's satisfaction and probate is adjusted accordingly, effective immediately."

She nodded to her court clerk, who rose and carried a document over to Pastore, where he sat at the table in front of the bar. "Mr. Pastore, as administrator of the estate, you're receiving a copy, but to save everyone's time, I'll summarize the pertinent portions *if* y'all will shut your traps!"

It was more effective than a gavel. April's neck prickled in the abrupt silence and she looked back again.

Jed was standing against the closed courtroom doors and he looked so good to her that it hurt.

His eyes met hers.

Her breath felt hard.

"The area known as Rambling Mountain," the judge continued, "excluding the boundaries known as Rambling Rad Ranch, is to be titled to the state of Wyoming for the purpose of establishing a state park." The statement earned another rash of commentary that she only quelled after several bangs of her gavel, and April was vaguely aware of the senator once more leaning in toward Squire.

When the courtroom was silent again, Judge Fernandez continued. "If the state is unwilling or unable to establish said park, the property passes to the Town of Weaver, again with the stipulation that the area is to be protected yet remain of public use. I'll forgo the legal land description, but in general he's referring to the mountain from somewhere just above the lake all the way down to the highway."

April saw Jed's eyes close.

She blinked hard. If Otis had made a point of separating out the ranch, he'd *had* to have planned for Jed to have it.

The judge's gavel pounded a few more times and she finally turned back around.

Snead had buried his face in his hands and she had the strong suspicion he was trying not to sob too loudly.

The judge continued. "The real property defined as the Rambling Rad Ranch—essentially from the lake to the summit—including all buildings and improvements and physical property—are to be sold forthwith." The words earned another whack of the gavel to silence the brooding eruption.

April, however, could barely fathom the words. She looked at Gage, who had a speculative look on his face.

"Preferably to the highest damn bidder." Judge Fernandez looked over her glasses again. "That's a quote, by the way. All proceeds from the sale go to Mr. John Edward Dalloway." She lifted her gavel yet again, then grimaced, as if realizing it was pointless. Her courtroom was in chaos. She leaned over her microphone again. "There are a few additional comments for Mr. Dalloway that I see no need to mention in this setting, and that's it."

"But I'm his *relative*!" Snead gathered himself enough to protest.

"That's it," the judge repeated loudly. "Mr. Pastore, I assume the auction of personal property that was stayed is still ready to proceed?"

"Yes, Your Honor."

"Good. Then I expect you to wrap things up quickly on that end. I'm sure you'll be busy entertaining offers on the real property soon enough. Adjourned." She stood up as the courtroom went wild and walked out.

When April looked again, Jed was gone. And she didn't even know if he'd stayed there long enough to hear it all or not.

Along with everyone else, she stood. Squire was thick in conversation with the senator and April looked up at her boss. She kept her voice as low as she could. "Get the ranch."

"April—"

"I know you think its value is minor compared to the rest of the mountain," she cut him off. "I don't care if it takes every penny I have. Just keep it under the company name like we'd planned before. Only this time it won't cost you a dime."

Gage looked pained. "You're really serious about that. A *guest* ranch?"

"Run by Jed, if he's willing. You offer it to him."

"Why would he keep working the Rad if he gets the money from the sale?"

"Just offer. Are we partners or not?"

His lips compressed. Then he nodded.

Satisfied, she worked her way around Snead, who'd become a sad slump in his seat, to push her way through the crowd and out into the corridor. There was no sign of Jed.

She hurried to the stairs leading down to the main floor and still couldn't spot him. When she made it outside to the sidewalk surrounding the building and still hadn't caught him, she leaned back against the stone wall, heaving a sigh of defeat.

She was still there when the stream of people exiting the courthouse dwindled. Her grandfather was one of the last.

"Never would have expected it of Lambert," he said when he stopped next to her. "Man never shared anything he didn't have to." His gaze was penetrating. "Your Jed's going to be a rich fella."

"He's not my Jed and he's not going to care about the money any more than I do. It's just giving him a bigger reason to leave." She could only hope that she was right and the ranch meant more to him. "What were you and the senator looking so thick about?"

"Lambert wouldn't deal on that pass I wanted, but state land is a different matter."

"Of course." Squire was always Squire. She pushed away from the wall. "I need to find Gage." It was an excuse. Her boss was probably already getting in the offer to Pastore. "We're flying back to Denver later this afternoon."

"Hmm." He tipped up her chin. "Try and see your grandma before you go. You missed the do on Memorial Day and she misses you."

April made a face. "She misses *you* and I wish the two of you would just end this stupid standoff!" Then, because no matter how frustrated she was with him, she loved him beyond measure, she pulled his head down to kiss his leathery cheek. "I'll be back for July 4 for sure," she promised thickly. "I expect to see both my grandparents there."

She hurried back inside the courthouse.

There was an elevator, albeit aging and slow, but she took the stairs again to the upper level, where most of the courtrooms were located, and as she'd hoped, she found her boss and Archer in deep conversation with Pastore and his curly-haired associate.

Aside from them, the courtroom had emptied.

Gage certainly didn't need her. She pushed through the doors and felt her knees actually go weak. "Jed."

He was standing in the corridor, a paper coffee cup in his hand. If he was surprised to find her still there or if he even cared at all was anyone's guess. His dark brown eyes were as unfathomable as ever.

She clutched the leather strap of her skinny briefcase. "You left the courtroom. Did you hear—"

"I heard."

She exhaled, feeling even shakier inside. "Otis was full of surprises, wasn't he? Turning around and doing what you said he'd never do? Leaving it for public use?"

"Yeah."

"You weren't entirely right about the rest. He might not have left you the Rad, but he did leave you what it's worth." She chewed the inside of her cheek. "Several million at the very least. You'll be able to go where you want. Do what you want."

"Appears so."

Her chest was aching and she fell silent. Looked back at the courtroom. "I don't want to keep you if you were going back in there. Nobody has more of a vested interest in what's being discussed in there than you. Pastore's got a copy of the will, too." She made her legs move, aiming for the staircase again. "You can see what else Otis had to say to you."

"Already know what he put in the will. Just came from talking to the judge." He pulled a folded sheet of paper from his back pocket. "Have my own copy now."

"Oh, well right." Her head bobbed mechanically. "Good." As anxious as she'd been to find Jed after the hearing was adjourned, she was even more anxious to escape now. She edged farther toward the stairs. "That's really good. Considering how old the envelope it was in, the will turned out to be pretty recent." It was an utterly inane observation.

"You saw for yourself. He kept everything in that cabinet. Apparently, even old envelopes. Why the hell he hid it away like he did is just one more Otis mystery."

She managed a genuine smile at that. But holding it for long was too hard. "I'm glad it's not going to drag on for you. The Rad won't languish on the market, that's for sure."

"Your boss not interested anymore?"

She managed to lift her shoulders. "He's got something up his sleeve. He's in there now with Pastore, making an offer. You should go talk with him." She gestured vaguely. "I think Squire's downstairs waiting for me." It was an outright lie and the tips of her ears burned even more because of it.

His voice followed her when she made for the stairs. "Don't you want to know what else he said?"

She sent him a look. "It's none of my business."

"It concerns you."

She stopped at that. "Since Otis wrote his will months before we even met, I know that's not true."

He closed the distance between them and held out the folded copy. "Take a look for yourself."

She obviously wasn't going to get out of there without a fresh new layer of torture. She took the paper from him, annoyed that she shivered when their fingers brushed, and slowly unfolded it.

It was brief. Just a few paragraphs, really. In handwriting that was shaky, but not so badly as to be illegible. The judge had gone in order, she realized, as Otis's first bequest dealt with the state park matter. The second, the sale of the ranch.

The last paragraph, though, obviously included the additional comments the judge had mentioned.

Ain't leaving the ranch to you, Jed, though I thought about it plenty. Don't want to see you end up like me. Too easy to hide away from things that matter when you're holed up on the side of a mountain. You were right about the Rambling needing sharing. I'm right about this. Take the money even though I know how you'll feel about it. You can give it all away like before, but I'm hoping you won't. The point of you is to go back out there and live a life worth living. Ain't nothing served by having your only companion be a past that's dead and buried. I should know.

Her vision blurred as she read the last line. "Your friend, Otis." She sniffed and handed the copy back to him. She forced a smile. "Told you that he was your friend." A movement behind them caught her eyes.

Gage and the others had come out of the courtroom. Archer and her boss spotted them immediately and headed their way. "A slightly unexpected twist," he greeted, quickly introducing Jed and Gage.

She avoided the glance that Gage flicked her way. "You all have things to discuss. I'm going to—" she waved her hand "—find the restroom." Before any of them could comment, she practically jogged away. Her heels sounded loud on the stairs. She was lucky she didn't land on her face, considering the way she raced down them.

The restroom was as much an excuse as finding Squire had been and she went straight out the exit.

Gage was her ride, but this was Weaver. Everything downtown was in walking distance.

The sun felt hot and she pulled off her jacket as she headed down the block. It didn't really matter where she went, as long as it was away from Jed. Eventually, she'd have to see him if Gage secured the ranch. But that would still take time.

She realized she'd reached Colbys when she walked right past it.

She backed up and went inside, going straight to one of the stools at the bar. She tossed her briefcase and jacket on the empty stool beside her and rested her forehead on her hand.

"I can serve you," Jane said, "but frankly, most of the folks coming in to drink this early in the day don't tend to look as classy as you. Hearing over?" she asked when April looked up at her.

She nodded. "Surprised the news hasn't already made its way in here. And I'll take whatever cola you have." She watched the other woman fill a glass with ice. "Nice of you to arrange the SUV for Gage."

Jane smiled. "Easy to be nice to Gage now we're not married." She set the filled glass on the bar top. "How'd it go?"

April told her the gist of the will.

"And Gage really wants to buy the Rad." Jane shook her head slightly as if it were hard to believe. Which, of course, it was. "Well, knowing him, he'll make a success out of it like he does everything else."

"Probably so." April was glad when a sizable group of women came in, chattering like magpies and pushing tables together, because it meant a distraction for Jane.

She pulled out her phone and sent a text to Gage

so he'd know where she was and dropped it back into her briefcase. She closed her eyes, rubbing her temples.

"You look like you've been pulled through a knothole."

April opened her eyes to see Piper standing there wearing summer shorts and a sympathetic look.

She got up and hugged her friend. "You said you were going to be in California with the youth group from your dad's church."

"They didn't need me as a chaperone, after all." Piper squeezed her hard. "Last thing I want to do now that school is out is herd a bunch of thirteen-year-olds seeing the beach for the first time in their lives." She pulled back to search April's face. "I heard about the hearing. How's Jed?"

April blinked hard and slid back onto the barstool. "Who knows?" Her voice was thick.

Piper sat beside her and bumped her shoulder companionably. "Everything's going to work out. Just because Jed is going to get the money instead of the ranch doesn't mean he'll just disappear or something."

"Turning into an optimist now?"

Piper smiled. "For the summer."

Jane was at the far side of the bar filling drink orders and April lowered her voice. "Gage is making an offer on the Rad."

"That guest ranch idea of yours?"

She nodded and quietly told her the rest and when she was done, Piper sat back.

"You don't look as surprised as I thought you would."

Piper gave her a look. "That you've found something you care about that much? What's surprising about that? Whether or not you think he'll never get over his wife, you're in love with Jed. When it comes to people you love, you'll do most anything. And I know that trust fund of yours is hefty, but won't turning the Rad into a guest ranch involve even more money?"

"Yes."

They both startled at the deep voice.

Piper pressed her lips together and widened her eyes at April. "Gotta go," she said suddenly, and hopped off the barstool to brush past Jed, hurrying through the breezeway that led from the bar to the family restaurant on the other side.

Which left April alone.

With him.

"You going to look at me or not?"

She did. Through the safety of the long narrow mirror on the wall opposite them. She felt hot all over, but her face looked pale. And unfortunately, even in the reflection, his gaze trapped hers. "How long have you been standing there?"

"Long enough."

Which told her absolutely nothing. She finally

managed to look away and lifted her glass, taking a gulp. "Did you talk to Gage?"

"He presented his idea."

Her hands felt shaky and she set the glass back down before she dropped it altogether. "And?"

"And it bears some thought. What are *your* plans?"

Confused and still wary, she frowned. "About what?"

"Going to go back to Denver? Plan your next development deal with Stanton?"

"*For* Stanton," she corrected, feeling even more wary. "It's my job. So—"

"Not planning to be involved in morphing a hundred-year-old cabin into a viable guest ranch if Stanton succeeds in buying the ranch?"

"Not really my forte." Her hands were tight as knots but she managed to keep her tone more or less calm. "Unless you're planning to head off for easier conditions with the money you'll be getting, you could still be the one running the Rad." She steeled herself. "Nobody would blame you if you washed your hands of ranching the hard way."

"I'm not still in love with my wife."

Her eyes snapped back to the mirror. Oh, she definitely had her answer now about how long he'd been standing there.

The women at the pushed-together tables were

laughing riotously about something and his brown eyes shifted away toward them for a moment.

She swiveled around to face him. Her chest was tight. "I don't believe you."

His lips compressed. Then he gestured at the bar. "That paid for?" He didn't wait for an answer, but whipped out his wallet and tossed a few dollars on the bar top. "Come with me." He wrapped his hand around her upper arm, seeming oblivious to the jerk she couldn't quite hide.

She barely had the presence of mind to grab her briefcase as he pulled her out of the grill. His grip didn't ease when he paused briefly at the curb, and then jaywalked across the street.

She had to skip a few times for the rest of her body to keep up with her arm. They were aiming for the park. "Jed—"

"Don't talk right now, April."

Despite the turbulence inside her, she huffed. "I *beg* your pardon?"

They'd reached grass and he stopped abruptly, finally releasing her. "Have I ever lied to you?"

Her mouth opened. Closed. She shook her head.

"Then why think I'm lying about that?"

Her throat tightened. She held the briefcase in both hands in front of her. It was paltry protection against the pull of him. "You still have your wedding ring," she finally said.

His brows yanked together as he squinted at her. "What?"

She looked over his shoulder toward Rambling Mountain. Toward the Rad and his bunkhouse-for-one and that thick gold band in his bathroom with *Forever* etched inside. "Your wedding ring," she repeated thinly. "I know you still have it. I saw it right next to your toothpaste the morning after we…we—"

He swore under his breath and rubbed his hand down his face. When he looked at her again, his eyes were soft.

So soft, they made hers burn.

"Come on." Instead of shackling her arm, he took her briefcase from her and closed his hand around hers.

Resisting him took more willpower than she possessed and she walked with him across the grass. Around a young couple and their baby spread on a blanket and past a gaggle of teenagers tossing a Frisbee. He didn't stop until they reached the empty gazebo. He set her briefcase on the weathered wood and nudged her down to sit, though he didn't.

"I need to tell you about Tanya."

There was no hope of squelching her tremble. "No, you don't have—"

"I do." He propped his hands on his hips and studied her. "From the first time I saw Tanya, I wanted her. I was like the peasant—"

"You're not a peasant."

"Trust you to say that. You don't think anyone is." His eyebrows were lifted slightly. "Going to let me finish?"

She clamped her lips together.

"She was like the princess in the tower. We were the same age, but she was private schools and exotic summer vacations and I was public school and sweating alongside my dad all summer."

She sucked in her cheek between her teeth. Great. A fairy-tale love.

"I was ten when she kissed me. The fact that she'd done it on a dare by her friends only made me more determined to get her." He spread his hands, then dropped them. "And I did, but not until I'd scraped my way up from peasant to a position with Hampton-Tiggs and was pulling down seven figures. Until then, I was still the kid with dirt under my nails." His lips twisted. "Just because I loved her didn't mean I was blind to her. We were twenty-three when we married in the biggest damn wedding—" He broke off, shaking his head. "She liked playing the princess to the hilt and I was ambitious and driven." His eyes roved over her face. "We were already crumbling when everything hit the fan at Hampton-Tiggs a year later. There were months of investigations. Every time I turned around there was another deposition. Another hearing. I started working with the investigators, putting as much time in with them as I'd ever done with the firm. She wanted me to go to another investment bank. Then when I put all my money into a fund benefitting the victims, she moved out. But she was pregnant, and—"

She reached out, her fingertips grazing him. "You don't have to do this."

He closed his hand around her fingers and pressed them to his chest. "I may not have loved the princess the way I should have, but I loved the baby." His eyes flickered. "Babies. You already know she was texting me when she had the accident. What is the point of you? That was the last thing she ever said to me."

Her heart felt like it was cracking. *The point of you is to go back out there and live a life worth living.* Otis had said it in his will. "I'm so sorry. Nobody should say such a thing."

He bent his head and kissed her fingers. "Nobody should. It doesn't change the fact that if I had been at that appointment, she wouldn't have been driving and texting me about it. She wouldn't have died. There was no way we would have made it together, married." The look in his eyes was heartbreaking. "But losing two babies before we even knew there were two." The scar on his chin looked whiter. "That broke me."

Her vision glazed.

"Three years later, I met Otis. He was in Texas

because someone there had died. Maybe a relative of Snead's. Maybe someone more important to him. I don't know. He never said. But I do know he kept me alive that night when he didn't have any reason to do so. Maybe he recognized someone more miserable than he was. When he bailed me out after the bar fight, he said I could come and work at the Rad. And you know the rest." He tugged her to her feet and touched her chin, nudging it upward. "That wedding ring I keep was not mine. It was my father's. He said he'd love my mother forever, and he did."

She blinked and a tear spilled over.

He thumbed it away, smiling faintly. "Such a softy."

She sniffed. "I thought—"

"I know." His gaze still on hers, he lowered his mouth to hers. Kissed her softly.

Her knees went weak and her fingers somehow ended up looped in his belt loops.

He cradled her face. "Why're you staking Stanton's deal?"

She sagged. "He wasn't supposed to tell you!"

"Too bad. Why?"

It was too hard to pretend anymore. Not with his eyes searching hers, seeming to reach down into the very heart of her. "Because I love you," she said huskily. "And you need the Rad."

"Oh, baby." He exhaled slowly and pressed his

mouth against hers until she was quaking. "I don't need the Rad. I *need* you, April. You're *my forever.*"

She sucked in a shaking breath. Her heart was falling wide.

He threaded back her hair. "It's still going to take a while for the court to decide on the sale of the Rad and I don't want to wait a while for you. I'm not that same kid who crawled his way up a princess's tower, but that doesn't erase who I was. Even though I know you deserve better—"

"Stop."

He ignored her. "I'll follow you if you go back to Denver. And I'll keep following until you stop and let me catch you."

She let out a choked laugh. "Oh, Jed." She traced her finger down his jaw. Running it slowly over his scar. Then his lower lip. "You caught me weeks ago."

His arms tightened and she could feel his heart beating just as hard as hers. "Then you'll stay?"

"I'll stay."

"If you get the sale, the money goes back into the Rad. We'll make it work together or not at all."

She moistened her lips. "Partners."

"Wouldn't you agree that's what a husband and wife should be?"

She went still and stared up at him. "Are you proposing?"

"At the risk of committing good ol' Ken's error—"

She cut him off with a fervent kiss. "You're not Kenneth," she assured thickly.

"Damn straight." He smiled slightly. "Reed and Dalloway. Rad. What do you say?"

His chocolate eyes seemed lit from behind and everything she'd ever wanted was there for the taking. All she had to do was reach.

The Rambling Rad had stood for nearly a hundred years.

And so would they.

"I say *yes*, Jed Dalloway." She slowly pulled his head down to hers, tumbling willingly into whatever their future would hold. "Because you're *my* forever, too.

* * * * *

She smiled that dazzling smile. The one that drew him like nothing else could. "If you're not busy around five o'clock or so, I'd love your help in putting together the rocking cradle my brother Rex ordered for Tony. It arrived yesterday, and I tried to put it together, but it has directions a mile long that I can't make heads or tails of. Don't tell my brother Axel I said this—he's a wizard at GPS, maps and terrain—but give him instructions and he holds the paper upside down."

Ah. This was almost a relief. He'd put together the cradle alone. No chitchat. No old family movies. Just him, a set of instructions and five thousand various pieces of cradle. "I'm actually pretty handy. Sure, I can help you."

"Perfect," she said. "See you at fiveish."

A few minutes later, as he stood on the porch watching her walk back up the path, he had a feeling he was at a serious disadvantage in this deal.

Because the farther away she got, the more he wanted to chase after her and just keep talking. Which sent off serious warning bells. That Harrison might actually more than just like Daisy Dawson already—and it was only day one of the deal.

Don't miss
Wyoming Special Delivery *by Melissa Senate,*
available April 2020 wherever
Harlequin Special Edition books and ebooks are sold.

Harlequin.com